THE FENCE

Other Books by Robin Friedman

The Silent Witness
A True Story of the Civil War

How I Survived My Summer Vacation…
And Lived to Write the Story

THE FENCE

A Novel

Robin Friedman

iUniverse, Inc.

New York Lincoln Shanghai

The Fence
A Novel

Copyright © 2005 by Robin Friedman

iUniverse books may be ordered through booksellers or by contacting:

iUniverse
2021 Pine Lake Road, Suite 100
Lincoln, NE 68512
www.iuniverse.com
1-800-Authors (1-800-288-4677)

ISBN-13: 978-0-595-37220-1 (pbk)
ISBN-13: 978-0-595-81618-7 (ebk)
ISBN-10: 0-595-37220-1 (pbk)
ISBN-10: 0-595-81618-5 (ebk)

Printed in the United States of America

For my terrific father-in-law, Leo Friedman, who generously shared his stories of growing up in the Catskills.

CHAPTER 1

---▼---

Blue-green dragonflies whirred around them as he came closer, the whisper of their papery wings mixing with the loud rush of water. He was tall, with vanilla-blond hair and faint green eyes. Everything about him seemed pale, from his light-colored hair, skin, and eyes, to the fine layer of ashen dust coating his overalls.

"Wow."

Cassandra Schreiber and Esther Schreiber, fifteen-year-old cousins and best friends, stared at him as he climbed up the hill, and, except for that one word expressing their amazement, were speechless.

He hadn't noticed them yet. They were sitting in their usual spot, on their favorite craggy boulder, right below the waterfalls. He walked absent-mindedly in their direction, his eyes downward, focused on the rolled-up newspaper in his hands. He stopped suddenly and unfurled the newspaper with a loud crack. He was close enough that Cassandra could spot today's date, June 9, 1935, stamped in black ink across the top.

The abrupt noise from the newspaper made Esther gasp, and he finally looked up. For a few seconds, no one said anything. He gazed at them curiously, as if not believing they were there, and they gazed back at him, wondering who he was, and what he was doing in their secret meeting place.

He finally broke the silence. "Didn't think anyone would be here," he said in a voice that was confident, almost brash. "Wanted some privacy is all. Guess you did too."

Cassandra wasn't the tongue-tied type, but she found herself unable to come up with an adequate reply. Two fat bees hovered near her cheek. She waved them away impatiently and said, "We come here every afternoon."

She didn't like the way that came out at all.

"It's our secret meeting place," Esther added.

Cassandra glanced at her cousin. Well, she thought, at least I didn't say *that*. Why did Esther have to reveal that to this stranger?

He smiled. Cassandra had never seen anything like it. It wasn't just the corners of his mouth that turned up—his eyes crinkled, his cheeks curved inward, two distinct dimples appeared on either side of his mouth, and his whole face seemed to shout, "Look at me! Look at my happy smile!"

The effect made Cassandra want to smile too—it made her want to laugh out loud. The beginnings of a smile were forming on Esther's lips. But Cassandra fought the impulse and asked in as flinty a tone as she could muster, "Who are you?"

He bowed deeply. "Chip Ackerman, jack of all trades and master of none, at your service. Just got in this morning. Going to be working here all summer." He spread his left arm in a wide arc.

Cassandra blinked. "Here?" she asked. "At The Waterfalls?"

Chip nodded. "That's right, doll. I believe that's what I just said."

Cassandra's face flushed with embarrassment, but she said nothing. Men passed through the Catskills all the time looking for work. It was the Great Depression, and everyone needed a job. Pop relied on these passing strangers to help him with the hotel. But Cassandra had never seen someone so young, so good-looking, working for Pop.

"And what about you two?" he asked, placing a dusty boot on their boulder and leaning on his knee. "Whatcha doing here?"

Cassandra looked from his boot to his face. He was very close now, and she could see his green eyes were flecked with gold. They were clear and deep—like emeralds. Oh, stop it! she thought in annoyance, you're beginning to sound like one of those weepy women on *Backstage Wife*, a radio serial featuring much swooning over romantic lovers. It was one thing to listen to those shows. It was another thing to start thinking like that.

"We live here," Esther replied, smiling shyly. "My name's Esther and this is Cassandra. Our fathers own the two hotels—they're brothers. Cassandra lives at The Waterfalls and I live at Schreiber's." She pointed beyond the tall fence that surrounded them.

"Ah, you're natives, then," Chip said. He drew in a long breath of air, which made his chest rise and fall, and looked around appreciatively. Behind him, a golden-winged woodpecker tapped on a tree. "It's nice up here in the mountains. And a whole lot cooler too. I sure am happy to get out of the hot city for the summer." He let his gaze rest on Cassandra. "But the last thing I want to do is intrude on your secret meeting place. So I'll be leaving. Sorry to bother you." He took his boot off their boulder.

They watched him as he started to leave. After he'd taken a few steps away, Esther called out, "You can stay if you want, Chip! We were about to go home anyway. I've got to get back and Cassandra's got to help her father milk the cows."

Cassandra wanted to throttle her cousin.

Why not tell him *everything* while she was at it?

Why not explain the fence between their two hotels?

Why not tell him why she and Esther had to meet secretly in the first place?

CHAPTER 2

▼

"Nah, I should get back too," Chip replied. "Tell you what, though, I'll come back tomorrow." He gave them a parting smile and left.

The sun hovered just above the trees, filling the horizon with apricot-colored light and backlighting a jagged formation of clouds that resembled dark smudges of ink. Cassandra pretended to study the sunset and tried to forget his smile.

Esther's eyes gleamed. "He was so handsome!" she exclaimed dreamily.

Cassandra couldn't disagree, but she wasn't about to say anything.

Esther grabbed her arm. "And he's working at your hotel!"

Cassandra shrugged. It would have made more sense for him to work at Esther's hotel. Esther was more ladylike, and he probably liked that delicate type. Esther, with her milky skin, cornflower-blue eyes, and dark curls.

Cassandra, on the other hand, was mostly brown. Her tanned face matched the honey-brown shade of her hair and eyes, as well as her fingernails, which were permanently rimmed with half-moon circles of caked dirt. Whenever she sat down, gritty plumes of dust flew into the air. And her thick hair never quite stayed in its long braid, dancing in flyaway wisps around her face instead.

Cassandra and Esther had been best friends since before either of them could remember. Cassandra's family lived at The Waterfalls, a small hotel with a shimmering green pond. It got its name from the waterfalls nearby, where Cassandra and Esther met secretly nearly every afternoon. Before becoming a hotel, it was a dairy farm, and it still had a big red barn, chicken coop, and eight black-and-white cows. The large white farmhouse, which had been expanded over the years, had four floors and accommodated 85 guests.

Esther's family lived at Schreiber's, a hotel that was newer, bigger, and shinier than The Waterfalls. It had a glistening swimming pool and casino where guests played poker late into the night.

The hotels were separated by a fence Pop built—something no one ever talked about. Not Bubbe, Cassandra's grandmother, who was Mama's mother and still lived with the family after Mama perished in the fire. Not Bela, the headwaiter at The Waterfalls, who'd worked there since before Cassandra was born. And certainly not Pop.

The girls said their good-byes and parted for the evening. As Cassandra ran down the hill to her hotel, she wondered, as she always did, what Mama would have done. What would Mama have done if an astonishingly handsome boy from New York City suddenly materialized out of thin air at the waterfalls?

Cassandra had blurry memories of Mama. She'd died when Cassandra was five. But Cassandra still thought about her mother—constantly and often.

Cassandra dashed toward the barn. She was greeted by the sweet scent of hay mixed with the sour odor of manure. Pop was already seated upon his stool in faded overalls with his "milking fedora" tilted jauntily to one side of his head. Most farmers did not wear hats while milking—especially fedoras—but Pop always did things his way.

"Hi, Pop," Cassandra said, grabbing a milk pail and seating herself beside him. "Come, Bossie," she urged softly, the way Pop always did. She arranged her pail under the large animal and squeezed the teats in the rhythmic motion she'd learned when she was small. Frothy streams of warm milk shot into the pail.

"Well, hello, there, *ziskeit!*" Pop exclaimed, his thick eyebrows wiggling like two hairy caterpillars.

Cassandra blew a bothersome strand of hair out of her eyes. "Um, Pop, how many men have you hired for the summer?" she asked casually, as if this was the kind of question she asked Pop on a regular basis.

Pop frowned, which Cassandra took rightly as suspicion. "Half a dozen or so. Why?"

Cassandra made her expression innocent. "Oh, I was just wondering." A mosquito whined in her ear. It wasn't safe—asking Pop these questions—but she went on anyway. She had to know. "Do you remember hiring a boy with, um, blond hair and green eyes?" A beautiful boy, she thought, the most beautiful boy in the whole world…

Pop gave her a curious look. "Not really, *ziskeit*. Do you know his name?"

Cassandra pretended to think. At last, she said, "Chip. Yes, Chip Ackerman."

Pop frowned more deeply. "Yes, I remember hiring him."

"What sort of work will he be doing, Pop?"

"And, might I inquire, dear daughter," Pop asked, his eyebrows raised to the ceiling, "why you are so interested in this particular worker?"

"I'm not interested!" Cassandra exclaimed a bit too quickly.

Pop made a *harrumph* sound. "He was hired to do odd jobs," he replied stiffly, then added, "And I don't want my little girl hanging around the people I hire."

"I'm not little," Cassandra mumbled.

The rest of the milking passed in silence. The only sounds in the barn were the splashes of milk into pails, the occasional mooing of a cow, and the increasing chorus of meows from the barn cats, who Cassandra always left with a saucer of fresh cream. Cassandra didn't mind the quiet. Her father wasn't the chatty type anyway. Besides, it gave her all the time she needed to think about Chip…

After milking, Cassandra made her way back to the hotel. The trees were fading into shadowy silhouettes around the algae-filled pond and a fine mist floated above it. A frog scissored lazily across the water. All Cassandra wanted to do was grab something to eat at the hotel and return outside to sit by the banks of the pond. She could stroll into the hotel kitchen at any time of the day or night and get anything she wanted. She'd always had the run of the place—The Waterfalls was like a huge playground to her. But Bubbe spotted her sneaking in.

"*Sheyne meydele*, look at you, you're a mess!" she cried, her tongue clucking in disapproval. She reached out and touched Cassandra's snarled hair. "Your hair, all tangled up like a bird's nest. *Feh*! If your poor mother could see you now, *oy gevalt*, what would she think?"

Cassandra hated when Bubbe said things like that. She liked to think Mama was a tomboy like her, unconcerned with combing her hair or keeping her fingernails clean. Mama had grown up in the mountains too, and Cassandra liked to think she prowled the woods and fields without a single care about her appearance.

In fact, Cassandra had trouble believing Bubbe was Mama's mother. They were so different. Bubbe was round and soft, with a bosom that stuck out like a shelf, and hair the color of ground cinnamon. She had immigrated to the Catskills from a tiny *shtetl* in Russia, and didn't like being outdoors at all.

In contrast, in all the pictures Cassandra had seen of Mama, her mother was as skinny as a string bean and always disheveled, as if she'd been in the middle of climbing a tree or exploring a gully before being pulled into the picture. Cassandra was sure Mama would have no problems at all with her messy hair or dirty fingernails. If Mama were here, she'd have messy hair and dirty fingernails too.

"You wash up," Bubbe said sternly. "Now."

"But, I'm hungry, Bubbe," Cassandra protested. That ought to get Bubbe's mind off washing up, she thought gleefully.

"Hungry? Why didn't you say so?" Bubbe exclaimed. She made Cassandra sit and loaded a plate for her with plump cheese blintzes, a mound of baked noodles sprinkled with cinnamon sugar, and a generous helping of carrot *tzimmes*. As Bubbe piled the plate, Cassandra studied the photograph of President Roosevelt that Bubbe had cut out of the newspaper and pinned above the counter.

"A good man," Bubbe always said about the president. "He will take care of everything." Like many Americans, Bubbe often wrote letters to President Roosevelt and Mrs. Roosevelt asking for help when neighbors needed warm coats or new shoes. She looked upon the president and first lady as people who were immediately concerned with her problems. That was why President Roosevelt and Mrs. Roosevelt were so popular, because most Americans thought of them as their personal friends in the White House.

Bubbe set down the plate in front of Cassandra. Cassandra ate slowly. Bubbe's cooking talents were renowned and everything was delicious. But if she gobbled it up too quickly, Bubbe would just load her plate again, and again, and again. Doling out second, third, and fourth helpings was Bubbe's pastime.

Bubbe made herself comfortable in the seat next to Cassandra. The Philco radio on the counter was broadcasting one of President Roosevelt's fireside chats. The president's fatherly, soothing voice filled the kitchen. "I want to talk for a few minutes to the people of the United States about banking," he said.

As a candidate, President Roosevelt had promised a "new deal for the American people" that would lift them out of the Great Depression. On Inauguration Day in 1933, Cassandra had crowded around the radio along with Pop, Bela, and Bubbe to hear him talk about what America might expect from that promise.

"So, first of all, let me assert my firm belief that the only thing we have to fear is fear itself," he'd started, "nameless, unreasoning, unjustified terror which paralyzes needed efforts to convert retreat into advance..."

And Cassandra knew from the way the grownups had reacted afterward that she'd just heard a speech of a kind no president had given since President Lincoln gave the Gettysburg Address.

Pop had even taken to singing a song he'd heard from someone passing through recently:

Mr. Roosevelt, you're my man!
When the times come I ain't got a cent,
You buy my groceries and pay my rent,
Mr. Roosevelt, you're my man!

Bubbe listened to the president speak for a few moments, then turned to Cassandra. "*Tsu gezunt*," she said pointedly.

"Sorry," Cassandra said. "Thank you."

Bubbe smiled, showing a row of crooked teeth. "You're welcome," she said again. Then she added, "When you're done eating, wash up and help Bela with the silverware."

"But, Bubbe!" Cassandra wailed. "I want to go outside."

"You've been outside all day. What more is there to see outside?"

How could Bubbe say that? Cassandra could spend the next *year* outside and still not see everything there was to see.

"Besides, it's getting dark," Bubbe observed.

"I just want to sit by the pond."

"Why? What for?"

"I like to think there."

"What does a little girl like you need to think about?"

"I'm not little," Cassandra groused for the second time that day. She finished eating and stood up.

"You help Bela now, *sheyne meydele*," Bubbe said.

"But, Bubbe—"

"Don't be a *nudnik*. He's waiting."

Cassandra sighed. She walked to the other side of the kitchen where Bela the headwaiter was sorting silverware. She washed up, then joined him.

"Hi, Bela," she said listlessly.

Bela, who was from Russia too, had watery grey eyes that Cassandra imagined were bright when he was a young man. Though he was nearly bald, rebellious tufts of snow-white hair still clung to his head.

"Hello, young lady," he said. "Why so downcast?"

"Oh, it's nothing," she mumbled.

Bela studied her for a minute. "Well, I'm going to tell you something you don't know. Something you never knew about your name. That ought to take your mind off things. Get you thinking about other things."

Cassandra was used to Bela's penchant for speaking in riddles. "My name?" she asked. "What do you mean?"

Bela gazed at her. "Cassandra isn't a Jewish name, you know. But your mother gave it to you for a reason, young lady. It's from Greek mythology, and, believe me, it's most fitting. How about that?"

Cassandra frowned. She had no idea what Bela was talking about. She supposed she could get interested in this topic, since it involved Mama, but she wanted to think about Chip—especially the possibility of seeing him at the waterfalls tomorrow.

"It's nice," she answered absently.

Bela chuckled. "I suppose it is nice. But, well, it's not nice at all when you really think about it."

Cassandra's eyes widened. "Not nice? Why?"

But Bela didn't have a chance to answer, because Bubbe frantically called him into the kitchen right then, and nobody ever refused Bubbe's call, especially when it was frantic.

CHAPTER 3

▼

Every summer, thousands of New Yorkers escaped their oppressively hot walk-up apartments and the teeming streets of the city to head for "the country." Many vacation postcards emphasized the cooler mountains. Cassandra's favorite read:

> *Don't Suffer When the Mercury Soars.*
> *Come Here.*
> *Be Cool Out of Doors.*

The musicians arrived. Sonny Grossinger and his Band of One Thousand Melodies would stay the whole summer and perform dance music every night. They would also be *tummlers*—social directors who performed skits and organized special events like the Masquerade Ball at the beginning of August.

The chauffer arrived with his navy-blue Cadillac that seated seven. His job was to ferry guests to and from the train station in Ellenville. He also took guests on daytime excursions to the reservoir or old prison.

Kitchen staff were hired to help Bubbe and Bela prepare food. They spent hours making *borsht*, chopped liver, and boiled beef. Guests were encouraged to eat as much as they wanted—three meals a day, all you could eat—plus tea and Bubbe's apple strudel and Chinese almond cookies every afternoon.

Pop paid his staff $11 a week. They got free room and board, and became part of the family for the summer.

The New Yorkers who came to The Waterfalls were cutters, needleworkers, furriers, and patternmakers who toiled in the sweatshops of the city's Garment District, saving their money all year round to spend a season in the mountains. The cost was a stretch for most of them, especially during these hard times, but it was the highlight of their year, and it let them escape from the crowded, sad help-lessness of the Lower East Side, a place that reminded them of the ghettos they'd tried to leave behind in Eastern Europe.

During the winter, Cassandra's family made ends meet by selling cheese and milk to the creamery at 10 cents a quart, tapping sugar maple trees for syrup, and selling eggs. Having a good summer season was important for making it through the colder months.

Every time Cassandra set foot in the kitchen, she was drafted to help. She diced onions, stirred broth, and stuffed *kreplach*, all the while gazing forlornly at the blue sky outside. The only good thing about being stuck there was that Bubbe never turned off the Philco radio. Cassandra liked listening to her favorite programs, especially *Little Orphan Annie*, but still vowed to avoid the kitchen as much as possible.

Men continued to pass through looking for work. Pop gave a grizzled, long-whiskered man the job of chicken plucking. The man slept in a tent on the far side of the pasture instead of the hotel, because the last chicken plucker had given everyone chicken lice.

The men working for Pop wore shabby suits with frayed collars, worn shoes with thin soles, and had teeth missing. Cassandra knew they'd left homes and families all over the country to find work. In their old cities, they'd gotten up every morning before dawn, washed, shaved, dressed as neatly as possible, and headed to the factory gates, only to find a hundred others already there, staring blankly at a sign that read, *No Help Wanted*. Cassandra had even heard a song about it.

> *I don't want your millions, mister,*
> *I don't want your diamond ring,*
> *All I want is the right to live, mister,*
> *Give me back my job again.*

"These hard times will end one day," Pop always told Cassandra. "President Roosevelt's New Deal will work. In the meantime, everyone can use a helping hand."

Pop had even given free room and board last summer to two men from the Federal Writers' Project, a special work program for writers by President Roosevelt's WPA, the Works Progress Administration. The men were working on an *American Guide* volume, the state-by-state guides that were being written for each of the 48 states, and asked Pop lots of questions about the Catskills.

Although Cassandra hated working in the kitchen, she liked helping with outdoor chores like feeding the chickens and milking the cows. A misty fog hung over the mountains the next day, shrouding their peaks in cloudy veils, when Cassandra made her way to the chicken coop. She scattered the hens' breakfast of dried corn in the yard and laughed as they pecked furiously at the ground.

The air felt damp and cool. Cassandra breathed deeply. She smelled mint growing thickly amid buttercups and clover. She leaned against the chicken wire surrounding the coop and wished she could spend all day outside. But school hadn't ended yet—thank goodness it would be over soon.

As she watched the chickens, time passed without Cassandra realizing it, and she had the strange feeling someone was watching her. Sure enough, when she looked up, she saw Chip by the barn, staring in her direction.

He waved. Cassandra felt a small thrill tickle her insides. She waved back self-consciously, finally noting the time, and hurried to the barn. She stopped short in front of Pop.

"Um, morning," she said awkwardly, taking a step backward.

Pop nodded. "Morning, *ziskeit*. Late today, I see."

"Um, yes," Cassandra replied absently. Her eyes darted around.

"It's all right, *ziskeit*. I have help this morning. You should get ready for school."

Chip stepped from behind Pop holding two pails in each hand.

"*Ziskeit?*" Pop asked slowly. "Didn't I tell you to get ready for school?"

"Oh, um, yes," Cassandra mumbled in embarrassment. She left the barn, walked to her bungalow, and tried not to think about what just happened. She washed and dressed quickly.

She and Bubbe shared a bungalow behind the hotel. It had two tiny bedrooms and an outhouse in the back. They had electricity, but no running water or heat. Pop lived in the bungalow next door, the one he used to share with Mama. In the winter, the family moved into the hotel, which was heated.

The bungalows were painted white with green trim, because white and green paint were the cheapest. Pop had built the bungalows himself from pine. There were five altogether. The three other bungalows were for guests, and they had front porches with Adirondack chairs, where guests liked to sit, smoke, and *kibitz*.

Guests paid $125 for the season to stay in a bungalow or $90 to stay at the hotel. The hotel rooms were tiny, and guests had to share bathrooms. There was just enough space for a bed, cot or crib, and dresser. Because the large farmhouse had been expanded over the years, there were strange connections between different wings of the hotel, and sometimes a series of steps going up or down where the old and new connected.

When Cassandra was ready, she headed to the hotel for breakfast. Bubbe would already be there. Her grandmother awoke at 5 a.m. every morning to light and stoke the wood-burning stove in the kitchen. In fact, Bubbe never seemed to rest. Even when she had time for an afternoon nap, she often worked in her garden on her knees instead.

Cassandra knew Bubbe wouldn't draft her to help this morning—thanks to school. Cassandra's breakfast was waiting for her on the kitchen table when she arrived, a soft-boiled egg and bowl of warm oatmeal with raisins and fresh cream. Having fresh cream every morning was one of the best things in the world about having cows.

On the radio, an excited announcer touted the benefits of Carters liver pills. Cassandra froze when she saw Chip filling the pitchers on the counter with cream. His flaxen hair sat in a messy heap on top of his head. It looked slipshod, though Cassandra could hardly criticize it, as her own hair was nearly always untidy.

What would it be like to run her hands through it? Would it feel silky against her fingers? Would it be soft?

The thoughts startled Cassandra. She'd never entertained such shocking ideas before.

His green eyes met hers—a glint of mischief in them. "Hope you didn't get into any trouble this morning on account of me," he said.

Cassandra felt her face burn. "No, of course, I didn't," she snapped. She focused on her breakfast, deciding to avoid his gaze, even though she could hardly taste a thing. When she finally looked up, though, he was gone. She felt an overwhelming rush of disappointment. Bubbe sank into the seat next to her holding a copy of the *Yiddish Daily News*.

"Burning books," she muttered. "These Nazis will stop at nothing."

Although Bubbe and Pop never discussed it with her, Cassandra knew they were worried about the Jews of Germany. A new government had come to power under a man named Adolf Hitler, and had recently banned Jews from serving in the German military. This week its newspapers called for a boycott of Jewish businesses. *Boykott the Juden!* the German front pages screamed.

Bubbe engrossed herself in reading her newspaper. Cassandra finished eating and stood. Without looking up, Bubbe said, "Don't forget to give your poor grandmother a kiss before you go, *sheyne meydele*."

Cassandra smiled. She quickly pecked her grandmother's cheek and headed outside.

The pasture was coated with a glittering blanket of morning dew. Insects skated on the surface of the pond, birds celebrated, and the guttural twang of a bullfrog rang through the air. Cassandra hurried to the meeting spot where Esther waited for her.

"You're late," Esther said.

"Sorry," Cassandra replied.

She wanted to tell Esther everything—about seeing Chip, about her name—but she held back. Normally, she never kept anything from Esther. She and Esther were like inseparable sisters. They knew where every huckleberry bush grew heavy with fruit, where vines sprawled with wild grapes, and where to gather all the hickory nuts and butternuts in the fall. They knew every fresh-water spring and locust tree and rabbit den.

Cassandra was glad Esther did most of the talking on their way to school. She let her thoughts wander as they passed pastures dotted with fluffy white sheep feasting on dandelions—scenes that belonged on picture postcards. By the time they reached the schoolhouse, Cassandra felt better.

Mrs. Rice taught the whole school in one room. It was a small building painted white with a big woodstove in the middle that crackled during the winter. The lower grades sat on one side of the room and the upper grades sat on the other side. Esther and Cassandra were in the tenth grade with three other students.

When the weather was good, Mrs. Rice held recess outdoors. The girls played jump rope and the boys played dodgeball. There were two outhouses in the schoolyard, one for girls and one for boys, and a well for getting a drink of fresh water. Each student had a cup hanging on a hook at the back of the room.

Cassandra took her seat next to Esther and waited quietly for Mrs. Rice to call up the class for their arithmetic lesson. A worn copy of *Silver Screen* slipped out of Esther's notebook. Fred Astaire, dashing in white tie and tails, and Ginger Rogers, resplendent in a feathered gown, peeked out from the cover. Esther planned to be a famous actress one day, and never went anywhere without her fan magazines. Esther slipped the magazine quickly back into her notebook before Mrs. Rice noticed.

"Tenth-grade arithmetic," Mrs. Rice announced. "Active position."

Cassandra's row immediately rose to their feet.

"Pass to the front," Mrs. Rice said. This meant the class was to sit on the recitation bench in front of Mrs. Rice's desk to recite their arithmetic lessons.

The school day passed uneventfully and Cassandra felt fine by the time Mrs. Rice rang the school bell at the end of the day. Mrs. Rice shut the schoolhouse door and walked to her black Chevrolet with the isinglass curtains. She was a terrible driver—she couldn't get the hang of shifting gears on the hilly roads of the Catskills—and her Chevrolet always bounced up the steep mountains like a grasshopper.

It was while watching Mrs. Rice drive away that Cassandra was suddenly reminded Chip was supposed to meet them at the waterfalls.

Would he really show up?

What if he didn't?

What if he *did*?

*   *   *   *

The girls made a beeline for the waterfalls. This wasn't unusual. But when they got there, they plopped themselves down on their favorite craggy boulder and waited.

And waited.

And waited.

And waited.

This *was* unusual.

Cassandra and Esther normally didn't wait for anyone, because nobody ever came to their secret meeting place.

And they were silent, which was *highly* unusual. Well, sometimes they liked to sit quietly and listen to the sounds of birdsong and rushing water. But, normally they talked nonstop.

Esther tapped her left foot incessantly while Cassandra nervously twisted her skirt. Her insides felt as tight as a ball of string. She forced herself to stop harassing her clothing and stroked the velvety-soft moss on the boulder instead.

"Why are we just sitting here?" she asked Esther.

"We always sit here," Esther replied. Cassandra detected a tiny touch of annoyance in her cousin's voice.

"Yes, but..." Cassandra countered, letting her voice trail off.

A cloud of gnats drifted past.

"Why don't we just go?" Cassandra asked.

Esther sighed. "I guess we should. He isn't going to show."

"You mean Chip?"

Esther blushed. "Yes, Chip."

"Do you like him?" Cassandra hadn't meant to ask this out loud, but she held her breath as she waited for her cousin's answer.

The girls heard footsteps. Esther sat up straight, fluffed up her curls, smoothed her skirt, and plastered a dazzling smile onto her face. She reminded Cassandra of a preening peacock she once saw on a farm.

Chip climbed up the hill toward them. Cassandra let out the breath she'd been holding in one long whooooosh.

"Well," he said merrily. "Told you I'd be back. And here's my harem, right where I left it."

Esther laughed. "We're not your harem," she said, but Cassandra could tell she liked the sound of that.

Chip smiled. "All right, then, my fan club. The Chip Ackerman Admiration Society."

"We're not your fan club either," Cassandra said in irritation. She got to her feet. "I'm going home."

Chip's smile disappeared, but his eyes still registered merriness. "Don't leave on account of me."

Cassandra narrowed her eyes at him. She wanted to say she was leaving precisely on account of him. Instead, she asked, "You coming, Esther?"

Esther barely glanced her way. "No, I'll stay here for a little while."

Cassandra frowned. "It's getting late."

"It's all right. You go on."

Cassandra shifted her weight from foot to foot, not sure what to do. When it was clear her cousin wasn't going to come, she turned away and sped down the hill without another word.

"Fine," she muttered to herself as she raced to The Waterfalls. "Let Esther stay. Let her giggle like a baby. He doesn't like me anyway. He likes her. And I don't like him!" She shook her head. "That's a lie. I do like him." She set her mouth in a hard line and repeated more firmly, "But he likes *her*."

She reached the pond, which resembled polished pewter, and stood there for several minutes, quietly admiring the peaceful scene. It calmed her. It always did. Feeling much better, she made her way into the hotel kitchen. As soon as Bubbe laid eyes on her, though, she was drafted to chop chicken for Bubbe's famous soup.

"Oh, why did I even set foot in here?" Cassandra asked herself. "I should have stayed by the pond." Then she thought of Esther, sitting by the waterfalls with Chip, and grew even more annoyed.

"Watch how you handle that knife, *sheyne meydele*," Bubbe scolded. "No need to slaughter the chicken again. It's already dead."

Pop swept into the kitchen carrying a stack of newspapers. "Have a look-see, everyone!" he roared. "Get your copy right here!"

Pop had bought advertisements in all the New York newspapers. Bubbe grumbled that it cost a "fortune." Pop sometimes advertised in *Summer Homes Among the Mountains*, an annual publication of the New York, Ontario and Western Railroad, but never newspapers.

"We'll be packing them in this year!" he shouted. "We'll bury the competition!"

Bubbe's mouth curled into a disapproving frown when he said that, but Pop didn't seem to notice.

"Take a look, Cassandra," he said, thrusting the page in front of his daughter's nose.

Cassandra peered at an advertisement that showed an artist's sketch of their hotel with the beautiful pond out front. Above the sketch, a headline read:

We may not have a casino.
We may not have a swimming pool.
But we have HEART.
We are the *haimish* place for your family.

Underneath that, the text read:

Excellent cuisine. Nightly entertainment. Homelike atmosphere. Beautiful surroundings. Milk from our cows. Eggs from our hens. Vegetables from our garden. Vacation paradise. Come join our family.

"It's nice, Pop," Cassandra said quietly.

"It's effective too, *ziskeit*," Pop said. "We'll beat 'em for sure this summer."

Bubbe looked up, her face contorted into an irate grimace.

"You want to see the ad?" Pop asked her.

"No, I most certainly do not," she answered stiffly.

Pop didn't respond. Cassandra thought Bubbe's strange reply might dampen Pop's enthusiasm, but he gave Cassandra a wink and, before leaving the kitchen, snatched a raisin cookie off a platter meant for arriving guests. Bubbe smacked his hand in mock outrage.

"Why didn't you want to see the ad, Bubbe?" Cassandra asked. "It was nice."

Instead of replying, Bubbe stirred the chicken soup so violently it splashed out and dripped down the sides of the pot. This was very unlike her. She reached for a towel and wiped down the spills in silence.

"Because it's a bad idea!" she suddenly cried. She scrubbed the counter ferociously as she spoke, as if there was some invisible stain on it that only she could see. "Just like your *tatte*! *Vai is mir*! Woe is me! Such *chutzpah*! And a waste of money. *Vos iz der tachlis*? What's the purpose? To hurt his brother?"

Her words tumbled out so rapidly it was as if they'd been locked in a safe for a century. "When will it end? Until everyone is ruined? *Vos noch*? What then? Do they want their children to carry on this nonsense after them? How I wish things were different. That I should see a change in my lifetime, I can go to my grave happy! *Verklempt*! *Se shtinkt*! *Um-be-shrien*! *Es vet gornit helfen*!"

When Bubbe got riled up, her Yiddish took over.

Bubbe gave Cassandra a look as if seeing her for the first time, and with a slight wave of her hand, said dismissively, "*Sheyne meydele*, you pretend you didn't hear anything I said. I forgot you were here. *Folg mich*."

Cassandra sighed. "I'm fifteen years old, Bubbe! When are you going to tell me about...the fence?"

Bubbe ignored the question. "Hurry up with the chicken. *Farshtaist*? The guests are coming, and they're going to be hungry!"

CHAPTER 4

▼

Summer at The Waterfalls always meant the sounds of mah-jongg tiles clicking in the dining room along with cries of "Five bam! and "Two cracks!" and the *clack-clack-clack* of men playing ping pong. Guests arrived by the trainload until the hotel almost burst at the seams.

"Merciful shade!" the wives cried when they beheld the thick forests of pine trees, drew deep breaths of air scented with wild roses, and saw stars for the first time in the night sky. Summer in the mountains gave them more free time than they ever had before. They read books, went for long walks, and had leisurely conversations with each other. Cassandra once overheard a boy tell his sister it was the first time he'd heard their mother laugh.

Some guests had been coming to The Waterfalls for so long Cassandra couldn't remember a summer without them. Mr. and Mrs. Rosenberg of the Bronx, for instance, were longtime guests who had definite ideas about meal times. Mrs. Rosenberg always drank three glasses of prune juice at breakfast; Mr. Rosenberg always asked for a small pitcher of liquefied chicken fat at supper to pour over his chopped liver.

But this summer had a different air about it. There were changes coming. Cassandra could feel it. When Cassandra arrived in the barn the next morning, she didn't need any more proof.

Chip sat in her usual spot. Cassandra stopped in mid-step, feeling a strange mixture of anger, confusion, and relief.

"Are you here again?" she asked.

Chip smiled. "I work here, darling. Remember?"

Cassandra glared at him. "No, *I* work here. And I'm not your darling."

"That's not what I hear."

Cassandra's mouth dropped. He was so impossible!

Pop entered the barn. He looked like he was on the verge of a friendly smile, but as his gaze drifted from Cassandra to Chip and back again, the beginnings of his smile vanished.

"Morning, *ziskeit*," he said a bit too politely. "I see you are here to help, but you need not for the rest of the summer." He smiled again, but it looked forced and out of place.

Cassandra frowned. "But I always help. I helped last summer, even though you hired Derrish."

Pop's smile stayed in place, but it looked strained. Cassandra could almost hear his thoughts, though he didn't say them out loud: "Derrish was from Poland, *ziskeit*. He could barely speak a word of English. Besides, Derrish was 66 years old, and this boy here, well, he isn't 66 years old."

Pop sat down carefully on his stool. "That is true, *ziskeit*, but this summer, you don't need to help."

Cassandra paused. "Not at all? Not even a little?"

Pop's phony-looking smile seemed like it was about to crack under the pressure. In a flash, he made it disappear off his face, then started fresh with a new one. "I will see you later, *ziskeit*. Have a good day at school."

Cassandra glanced at Chip, who'd been silently milking throughout this strange conversation, staring into his pail as though the secrets of universe were swirling inside it. This wasn't about helping Pop with milking. Cassandra knew that. And yet, she didn't know what it *was* about. She liked to help Pop, and loved the cows and barn cats and foamy pails of milk, but this had nothing to do with that. This had to do with Chip, and the way Pop talked to her when Chip was around.

Laughter drifted into the barn. Everyone turned to see a knot of guests standing at the doors. Every season, some guests woke while the sky was still a pale gold to visit the barn. These enthusiastic guests would grab a mug from the dining room on their way out the door and bring it to the barn so they could dip it into the milking pails for a taste of fresh milk. Guests who liked fresh milk also enjoyed wandering into the chicken coop to collect fresh eggs, and pulling up their own carrots, scallions, and cucumbers from Bubbe's garden. These were the guests who appreciated the fact that Bubbe's barrels of homemade sauerkraut were grown from the cabbages in her own garden.

Pop started on another smile, this new one an attempt to be warm and welcoming. He seemed exhausted from his efforts.

"Morning, everyone!" he said excitedly.

"Morning! Morning!" the guests called. They surged forward with their mugs. Pop hid his irritation as they dipped them into his pail.

"Right from the cow!" they exclaimed happily as they brought their mugs to their lips. "Still warm!"

The last thing Pop wanted to do was insult his guests or deny city dwellers a chance to experience the pleasures of farm life. But, at the same time, neither Pop nor Cassandra could understand how their guests drank unstrained milk that still contained bits of dust, dirt, and grit. Pop removed these impurities before serving any milk at the hotel by running it twice through strainers with cotton filters.

Still, the guests smacked their lips in approval, lifted up their mugs as if making a toast, and cried excitedly, "*Shum! Shum!*"

Neither Pop nor Cassandra knew what "*shum*" meant, but they gathered it had something to do with fresh milk. Cassandra guessed the cream, which always rose to the top, made the milk taste good even though it was gritty.

A troop of children wandered into the barn behind the guests, wide-eyed and speechless. Most had never seen a cow in their lives. Pop couldn't resist aiming a teat in their direction and squirting a spray of milk into someone's unsuspecting face. The milk flew in a stream across the barn like a white arrow, landing squarely in the middle of a boy's startled face.

After a moment of stunned silence, the barn erupted into giggles and shrieks of delight, and the children opened their mouths and begged for sprays in their direction.

Cassandra laughed. The arrival of the children and guests seemed to cheer Pop and lighten her own mood.

If Pop didn't wish her to milk this summer, she would accept that. She let herself look at Chip. He winked at her, and her stomach did a little flip, like an egg being tossed in a skillet.

*   *   *   *

Cassandra met Esther at their usual spot along the tree-studded path for the walk to school. It was their last day, and the pine-scented air filled Cassandra's lungs with a great sense of possibility. As she gazed at the maples and firs that dotted the countryside—ranging from bright emerald to deep jade—she couldn't help feeling that all was right with the world.

"So—tell me everything!" Esther exclaimed.

Cassandra blinked. "Everything about what?"

Esther made a show of sighing with great frustration. "You know. About *him*. Tell me everything!"

"Well, all right," Cassandra began slowly, not really sure what she should say, or more importantly, what her cousin wanted to hear, "he's going to help Pop milk the cows." This information seemed far from thrilling, yet it set Esther to a fit of giggles. Cassandra started to tell Esther about Chip's wink in the barn, and her stomach flip-flopping, but decided against it.

"I wish he worked at *my* hotel!" Esther cried dramatically.

"I hardly ever see him," Cassandra muttered, though that wasn't completely true. Cassandra ran into Chip far more than she expected, and yet, not far enough. The latter thought filled her with surprise.

"Well, at least you get to see him at all," Esther said.

The whistling of a quail pierced the air. They walked in silence and Cassandra tried to make sense of things.

Why had this city boy suddenly become so important to her and her cousin?

Well, because he was unbelievably beautiful, for one. He belonged in one of Esther's fan magazines. He belonged on the silver screen at the Rialto theater in Monticello.

And, he was, well, fun to be around. When he wasn't being insufferable.

And he was new. Anything new was good. Nothing changed much in the mountains.

There just weren't a lot of beautiful Jewish boys with blond hair and blue eyes exactly the right age around. Cassandra and Esther were both fifteen, but neither one had ever gone out with a boy or even kissed one.

Cassandra imagined her fingers entwined through Chip's vanilla-blond hair again. Then she dared to imagine his mouth on hers. But the thought was so outlandish, so crazy, she had to bite her lip to keep from laughing. She tried to picture Esther with him instead. It was easier.

They passed the Grand View Hotel, which had burned to the ground in 1913. There were so many fires in the Catskills. Another fire that same year had devastated the town of Liberty. And, in 1909, the big town of Monticello was almost destroyed by fire. Cassandra looked away from the hotel ruins. They reminded her of Mama dying.

"Pop showed me his newspaper advertisements," she said, breaking the silence, hoping to distract herself from her thoughts.

"Did he?" Esther replied absently. "Tell me—does he smile when he talks to you?"

"Who—Pop?"

"No, *him*."

"I don't know. Don't you want to hear about Pop's advertisements? Don't you want to know what he's…trying to do to Schreiber's?"

"Let's finish talking about *him* first."

"I thought we were finished."

"Of course not! Does he get those dimples when he smiles?"

Cassandra snorted. "Esther, don't you think Pop's advertisements are more important than his dimples?"

Esther paused, considering it. "I guess so. *Does* he get those dimples, though?"

Cassandra answered through gritted teeth, "Yes, he does. Two dimples on either side of his face. Happy, now?" Esther would probably grumble at her sarcasm, but, instead, Esther just repeated with a distinct air of drama, "I wish he worked at *my* hotel!"

They reached the schoolhouse, and Cassandra still hadn't told Esther about Pop's newspaper advertisements. She also hadn't told Esther about her name coming from Greek mythology or Bubbe's strange outbursts in Yiddish. The entire walk to school had been dominated by silly talk of *him*.

Something like this had happened last year. Cassandra had wanted to discuss *Sherlock Holmes*, but Esther was more interested in *The Romance of Helen Trent*, a ridiculous soap opera, and all Cassandra heard about for weeks was "bosoms rising" and "tender kisses" and whispered poetry so sappy it made her want to scream. Thankfully, Esther had come around to *Sherlock Holmes* in the end. Perhaps this was going to be like that. Esther probably needed time to get *him* and his dimples out of her system.

The last school day passed quickly. There weren't many lessons, and Mrs. Rice served chocolate cookies. Cassandra could feel the younger children's growing restlessness along with her own. She knew that as soon as Mrs. Rice closed the schoolhouse door for the season, there would be a tidal wave of excited children spilling into the schoolyard.

During recess, the other girls gathered outside for a game of jump rope, but Esther pulled Cassandra aside, a serious look on her face, and asked, "How old do you think he is? Can you try to find out?"

"Esther! For goodness sake! Fine! I'll try to find out!"

Esther bounced up and down on her toes like a little girl who'd just won a package of candy-coated caramel Sugar Babies. "And one other thing. Can you find out if he has a girlfriend back home?"

"Have you gone mad, Esther?" Cassandra asked, though she wanted an answer to that question too.

Esther turned pink. "I'm just curious."

Cassandra's mouth formed into a tight line. "Fine—I'll ask him. Now I need to see Mrs. Rice about something."

"But it's recess," Esther protested.

"Yes, I know, but it's important," Cassandra replied, then turned to go back inside the schoolhouse before Esther could stop her.

Mrs. Rice was sitting at her desk writing in a large notebook.

"Mrs. Rice?" Cassandra asked. "I was wondering if I could ask you something." She hadn't lied to Esther. She had something important to ask Mrs. Rice, and she needed to do it today, before school ended for the season. Of course, she also wanted to escape Esther's foolishness.

"Of course," the teacher answered, smiling. Mrs. Rice had dark red hair that was pulled into a tidy bun at the back of her head.

"My name," Cassandra said. "Do you know what it means?" She was about to add that it was from Greek mythology, but Mrs. Rice piped in, "Why, it's from Greek mythology, did you know that?"

"Yes," Cassandra replied. "But what does it mean?"

"Let's find out, shall we?" Mrs. Rice said. She got to her feet and turned to the cabinet behind her desk, which was called the library, because it was crammed from top to bottom with books. Mrs. Rice ran her finger across the book spines until she reached a thick book with a blue cover. She pulled it from the shelf.

"Here we are," she said. She flipped pages. "Aha," she cried, pointing a finger at the middle of the page. She read out loud, "Cassandra would foretell only truth, but no one would believe her."

Cassandra frowned. That hardly helped at all. "What does *that* mean?" she asked in bewilderment.

Mrs. Rice looked as though she'd been waiting her whole life for someone to ask this question. She shut the book with a loud snap and returned it to the shelf. "According to Greek mythology, Cassandra was given the gifts of seeing the future and telling only the truth. But—she was also given a punishment—that no one would believe her prophesies. So, even though all her prophesies were true, no one ever believed her."

Cassandra shook her head in confusion. What in the world made Mama choose this name for her? Is this what Bela meant when he told her it wasn't "nice"? What did this strange name have to do with anything?

Mrs. Rice eyed her curiously. "Does that help?" she asked.

Cassandra sighed. "Not really." She hadn't planned on telling Mrs. Rice, but she found herself saying, "My mother picked the name for me on purpose."

Mrs. Rice took her seat. "Ah," she said, as if she'd been there when Mama had chosen it. "Your mother thought you would see things clearly, but that no one would believe you." She suddenly looked thoughtful. "Your mother was optimistic about you, but pessimistic about everyone else."

CHAPTER 5

▼

School was finally over, and even though Cassandra took great pains to avoid Bubbe and her kitchen, she inadvertently found herself helping prepare stuffed *derma*, boiled *flanken*, and chocolate marble cakes over the next several days. And, before she knew it, the first Friday of the season—bringing Shabbos with it—swept into The Waterfalls.

Shabbos was the grandest day of the week at The Waterfalls. That's when Bubbe and her kitchen staff truly showed off their cooking talents with a lavish multi-course meal. Most guests made sure to arrive in time for Bubbe's Shabbos supper. Some even came as early as dinner. It all depended on whether fathers could convince their bosses in New York to let them have a few hours off on Friday.

Fathers arrived at the hotel every weekend by "Bull Train." It was a hard journey that never took less than six hours. First they had to cross the Hudson River at 42nd Street in New York City on the Weehawken Ferry. Once in New Jersey, they boarded the New York, Ontario and Western Railroad.

Fathers usually came Friday, and left Sunday to return to their jobs in the city. Wives and children stayed all summer. During the week, women ruled The Waterfalls. On weekends, the balance of power shifted. All week long, Cassandra heard mothers say to their children, "Just wait till I tell your father what you did when he gets here on Friday!"

Pop liked to kick off the first weekend of the season with a Dance Marathon. Although Sonny Grossinger and his Band of One Thousand Melodies played dance music every night for Pop's guests, Bela made the Dance Marathon extra festive by decorating the dining room with colored crepe paper. Some of the hotels in the Catskills were *frum*, religious, and men and women were not permitted to dance together. But not The Waterfalls.

Cassandra got caught up in the excitement of the dance preparations, as she always did. Besides, spending time with Esther had stopped being fun lately. Cassandra dreaded meeting her cousin on their favorite craggy boulder by the waterfalls.

"Well?" Esther prodded that afternoon as Cassandra made her way up the hill.

Cassandra sighed long and loud. "Esther, I haven't seen him. I promise I'll ask him. Things at The Waterfalls are busy."

Esther folded her arms across her chest. "Things at Schreiber's are busy too. You have to make the time, Cassandra."

"I haven't seen him!" Cassandra yelled, throwing up her arms. "He's busy. We're busy. We aren't fancy like your hotel. We don't have butlers in white jackets. We have to do everything ourselves."

Esther gave her a cousin a pouty look. "Well, at least he works at your hotel."

Cassandra turned away. "I wish he'd never come."

"Why?"

"I'm tired of talking about him, Esther!"

Esther paused. "What about those advertisements you were telling me about?"

Cassandra brightened. At last—her cousin was willing to drop all the nonsense about Chip and talk about important things. "They're really nice, Esther," she said, sitting down next to her cousin. "But Bubbe said they cost a fortune." She winced as she added in a low voice, "Pop said he would 'bury the competition.'"

Esther frowned. "I don't think my father is worried about that." She stared into the distance. "But I do wish they'd stop this stupid feud with each other…" She let her sentence trail off.

Cassandra nodded. It was something neither of them liked to discuss, but it was never far from their minds.

They fell silent as dragonflies flitted around them like jewels. Cassandra opened her mouth several times, but didn't know how to articulate her mixed-up feelings with words. She thought about starting with the revelation about her name, and what Mrs. Rice had told her about it. She also thought about telling Esther about Bubbe's Yiddish outbursts. Finally, she gave up on everything and said, "I should probably go."

Esther gave her a meaningful look.

"I know, I know," Cassandra said wearily. "I'll ask him."

"Not that," Esther mumbled. "Our fathers…those advertisements…the feud…oh…never mind."

Cassandra understood the difficulty of trying to explain something that made no sense. So, she simply squeezed Esther's hand, said good-bye, and started back down the hill.

         *   *   *   *

By evening, Cassandra was exhausted from all the helping she'd done. Still, she'd washed up, and dressed in her nicest white blouse and blue skirt, and even threaded a powder-blue ribbon through her hair. She'd thoroughly enjoyed Bubbe's split-pea soup with lots of crunchy *mandlen* in it, roasted chicken, buttered noodles, chocolate pudding, and lime Jell-O. Cassandra loved Jell-O—especially the Jell-O jokes she always heard on *The Jack Benny Show*:

Jack: *Hey, Mary, why is Jell-O like a fellow with two steam yachts?*
Mary: *Because it's extra rich!*

Sonny Grossinger and his Band of One Thousand Melodies had played a march to shepherd the guests into the dining room when the doors opened, and background music throughout the meal. Between the soup and entrees, though, the kitchen fell behind, and Pop called upon the band to help. They played *The Star-Spangled Banner*, and all the guests stopped eating and stood in respect. This gave Bela and his staff about five minutes to catch up. Of course, longtime guests like Mr. and Mrs. Rosenberg were wise to this trick, and knew what was going on whenever the band played *The Star-Spangled Banner*.

By the time the Dance Marathon began, even Bubbe had ventured outside the kitchen to admire the dancers. Cassandra watched, enthralled, as ladies in lacy, empire-waisted dresses with puffy sleeves and evening gloves twirled elegantly across the floor as the band played a rumba, moved on to a tango, then played a polka. Would she ever look like that? An image popped into her mind—she was dancing with Chip. She shook her head in alarm.

When the glamorous Feder Sisters—a raven-haired duo in flowing scarlet caftans whom the band had hired specially for tonight's dance—took to the stage to belt out *Schain Vi Di Livone* and other *freilachs*, *bulgars*, and *shers*, Pop launched himself onto the dance floor and began doing the *kazatzka*, a Russian dance from his youth. The crowd exploded into applause as he performed the strange, halting movements.

Then Pop, smiling and red-faced, started a conga line and asked everyone to join in. Bela obliged, as did Bubbe, and most of the kitchen staff, and practically all of the guests, and before she knew it, Cassandra had wrapped herself around her grandmother and joined in the festivities.

It took a moment before Cassandra realized that the person behind her, the one holding her waist, was none other than Chip, who was wearing the uniform of a busboy. She looked back at him, tingly and flushed with the thought of him actually touching her, and he winked at her for the second time, and, without thinking, she smiled. And, yes, when he smiled back, she noted that he definitely had two dimples on either side of his face.

"How about some fresh air?" he whispered into her ear, and she nodded, and found herself following him outside until they were standing by the banks of the pond. The water was satiny, shimmering like burnished silver, and the cheery chirps of spring peepers filled the air.

"You Catskills folks sure know how to party," Chip said.

Cassandra suddenly felt self-conscious about what she was wearing. She touched the ribbon in her hair and wondered if it made her look like a little girl.

"It beats the city on any old day," Chip went on.

It was then that Cassandra remembered that she was supposed to ask this boy a list of questions. She didn't know how she was going to do that, what with feeling so shy and hot at the moment, but she had promised Esther. So, she cleared her throat, and asked, "How old are you?"

"Sixteen. Who wants to know?"

She ignored his question and asked, "Do you have a girlfriend back home?"

"Whoa, sister," he protested with a laugh. "And what if I do? Does that ruin all your dreams?"

He was joking, she knew, but the sharpness of his unexpected taunt bothered her.

"No," she replied coolly, tossing her hair. "But it might ruin yours." This was how women on those radio serials talked—sassy and smart and brazen.

"Is that so?" he answered, taking a step toward her.

Was he going to…

Cassandra's heart skipped a beat, and her eyes fluttered to a close. But, no, she'd imagined it, because when she opened her eyes a moment later, Chip was staring across the glassy surface of the pond. He sunk his fingers gently into the water, creating thick ripples that ruffled away like molasses.

"It's so beautiful up here," he murmured.

"Yes," Cassandra said. "I love it." At the mention of the word "love," she felt her cheeks burn.

"And, no, I don't have a girlfriend," he said. "The position is wide open. In fact, applications are now available."

Cassandra rolled her eyes. He was so cocky, so full of himself, so impossible, yet she was drawn to him like the pull of a tide. She wondered sheepishly what sorts of questions he'd ask on an application for a girlfriend.

How would she score on it?

And who would score higher—her or Esther?

She was more disappointed than she wanted to be when he said, "I better head back inside before your father thinks I skipped town."

CHAPTER 6

▼

"Last night, at midnight, I got KDKA in Pittsburgh on the radio dial," Pop announced to his guests three days later as they dug into their lox and eggs and smoked fish. "And here's the news."

With great flourish, he began reading from a sheet of paper. "Babe Ruth has retired from professional baseball with 714 home runs...The *S.S. Normandie* has broken the record for crossing the Atlantic Ocean at 107 hours, 33 minutes..."

It was small touches like that—giving his guests the latest news at breakfast—that made Pop such a wonderful host.

"Cassandra, my goodness, you just get prettier every summer!" Mrs. Rosenberg gushed as Cassandra poured her a third glass of prune juice.

Cassandra blushed, looked away, and murmured an embarrassed "thank you."

"Soon you'll be driving all the boys crazy," Mrs. Rosenberg went on.

Cassandra's blush deepened. She didn't know about all the boys, but if she could just catch the attention of one boy in particular...

After the guests had cleared out of the dining room, Cassandra helped Bubbe lead a clamoring crowd of children in arts and crafts. Bela hovered over the group, frowning, as everyone fashioned tiny ashtrays out of clay. Poor Bela—the children were making a mess—and he had to set the dining room for dinner.

Sometimes Pop talked about building an extra room at The Waterfalls, so the dining room didn't need to be used for so many activities. Esther's hotel, Schreiber's, had extra rooms. But Pop had never been able to afford it.

The Great Depression had brought hard times for everyone ever since the stock market crashed in 1929. Thousands of banks had failed and many people had lost their entire life savings. Few banks were lending anymore, and even the

Jewish Agricultural Society, which had given Pop credit over the years, had little money these days.

Cassandra knew her family was luckier than most. At least her family lived on a farm and could feed themselves. The hotel cows gave milk twice a day. Bubbe and Bela could make all the butter, sour cream, cheese, and sweet cream they needed. The chickens gave eggs every day, and Bubbe's garden provided vegetables. Whatever Cassandra's family couldn't grow, they could get by bartering. Whenever Pop went into town, he traded milk, eggs, and cheese for sugar, salt, coffee, tea, and bread.

Cassandra knew her family, like most hotel owners, lived hand to mouth. They existed on credit, had no savings, and made no profits. But at least they had a place to live and food on the table.

"Bubbe, how did you and Zeyde meet?" Cassandra asked as she stopped a little boy from smearing his mouth with clay. Cassandra had fewer memories of Zeyde than she had of Mama. The memory she most closely associated with her grandfather was the sweet aroma of his smoking pipe.

"The *shadchan* made the match for us," Bubbe replied. "We didn't meet until our wedding day."

"Really?" Cassandra chirped. "What about Pop and Mama?"

"Your mother and father met in school," Bubbe answered absently. "What is it with these questions, *sheyne meydele*? Are you planning a summer romance?"

"No," Cassandra sputtered, feeling her neck go on fire.

Bubbe gave her a long look. "But you are almost all grown up now, yes, I do see that," she murmured. "Not so much a *pitseler* anymore."

Cassandra turned away in embarrassment and wished she'd never brought it up. She stopped another boy from running his clay-drenched fingers through his hair.

After arts and crafts ended, Bubbe headed to the kitchen with an intense look on her face, a look that meant she was intricately planning tonight's supper menu.

"Chilled melon, matzo ball soup, sponge cake…" she recited to herself.

This list-making served as a serious warning to Cassandra. If she didn't make herself scarce, she'd be stuck rolling matzo balls for the rest of the day. She ran outside before Bubbe noticed.

The air smelled sweetly of honeysuckle, and the pleasant twittering of birds filled her ears. A group of children rocked noisily on the wooden seesaw Pop built last summer. Another group of children gathered around the well hand pump. City kids found the well hand pump fascinating, and often held contests to see who could pump up the most water in the quickest time. They loved to drink the cold, delicious water.

Cassandra headed automatically to the pond, but slowed down when she saw someone sitting by the banks.

Chip.

She hadn't seen him lately. Even if she wanted to avoid him, she probably couldn't. She considered turning around, but it was *her* pond, after all. She'd sit there if she wanted.

He smiled at her—dimple-filled as always—when she reached him. "This is one of my favorite spots," he said.

Cassandra replied, "Mine, too. I especially like how it changes. Sometimes it's green, sometimes it's grey. It's like the pond has moods." She instantly hated the way she sounded. Why had she gone on like that? He was a city boy—he didn't care about such things.

But Chip said, "Hey, I like that."

They quietly admired the silky surface of the silvery water.

"Why are you here?" Cassandra asked bluntly.

"I got some time off this morning," he answered.

"Oh," Cassandra said. A thought began filling her head.

"Hey, what do you do for fun around here? Maybe you could show me a good time."

It had been her thought exactly. "Well," Cassandra said shyly. "I'm meeting Esther soon."

"At your secret meeting place?" he teased, smiling at her.

Cassandra smiled back. Oh—he was so handsome! She wished she could touch his face. "Yes. We're hiking up to Dead Man's Gorge today."

"Hey—that sounds fun. Mind if I tag along?"

Cassandra had to stop herself from blurting out that she didn't mind at all. Instead, she said as casually as she could, "That's all right, I suppose."

Chip got to his feet and dusted off his pants. "Then I'll meet you by the waterfalls in a little while." He winked at her.

Every nerve ending in Cassandra's body went on alert. She was sure he meant nothing by that, and yet, at the same time, she hoped he did. She raced up the hill toward the waterfalls, the tips of her fingers tingling.

Esther was waiting for her on their boulder, engrossed in the latest copy of *Picture Show*, which featured her favorite movie star, Clark Gable, on the cover. Cassandra plopped down next to her, sending clouds of dust flying into the air as if announcing her arrival.

Esther put down the magazine and fanned the dust away from her face. "For goodness sake, Cassandra, can't you *try* to be less dirty?"

It reminded Cassandra of Bubbe's tirades for cleanliness, but even that failed to dampen her excitement.

"He's coming," she whispered excitedly. "He's coming with us."

"Who's coming?" Esther asked, still waving dirt from her face.

"*Him!*"

"*Him?!*"

Her cousin's blue eyes rounded like marbles. She looked panicked for a moment, then frantically combed her fingers through her dark curls. "Wish you'd told me," she muttered.

"Oh, you look fine, Esther."

"Yes, but I wish I'd known ahead of time. When's he coming?"

"In a few minutes."

"Oh, my. I really wish you'd told me."

"Esther, will you please calm down?"

Esther suddenly looked serious. "Cassandra, we've got to talk."

"About what?"

"Well, see, there's only one of him, but there's two of us. So, one of us is going to have to be mature about it."

"Mature? Mature about what?"

"Mature about him choosing the other one."

Cassandra was thunderstruck. Would it really come to that? "What if he doesn't like either one of us?" she asked softly.

Esther ignored the question, pinching her cheeks to make them rosy. "We've got to make a pact. We'll stay best friends no matter who he chooses."

Cassandra mumbled, "I wish I'd never told him to come with us. I wish he'd never come here at all." And, at that moment, she believed that. Chip was fascinating, but he made things between her and Esther feel strange, confusing, *dangerous*.

"I think it's quite exciting," Esther said, smoothing her skirt. "Besides, love isn't something you can control."

"Love?" Cassandra grunted. "You've been listening to way too many soap operas, Esther."

"Love is real, Cassandra," Esther said.

Cassandra threw up her hands. "For crying out loud, Esther, I knew he'd come between us!"

And with that comment still hanging in the air, Chip appeared at the top of the hill.

*   *   *   *

The girls gazed at him with mouths agape.

"Bad timing?" he asked.

Esther plastered a smile onto her face. "No," she said sweetly. "Perfect timing."

She walked to where he stood, and to Cassandra's shock, took his hand and led him to the boulder, where she made him sit down next to Cassandra. Cassandra gave Esther a dirty look as her cousin stood in front of the two of them. Cassandra recognized the stance—her cousin was about to give a performance.

"Cassandra gets to see you so much more than I do," Esther pouted in a way Cassandra decided was extremely unbecoming. "It's so unfair. Just because you're working at The Waterfalls. So, sit here and tell me all about yourself."

Chip grinned. "Not much to tell. Besides, I thought we were going hiking."

Esther made a face. "Oh, pooh, that's something Cassandra likes to do. I mean, I like being outdoors too, but, well, don't you think hiking is unladylike?"

Chip let out an amused laugh. "Somehow I don't think I'm the best judge of that."

Esther sighed dramatically. "Oh, well, why don't the two of you go hiking without me. I'll just be on my way." She started taking baby steps forward, peering at Chip over her shoulder in a way those radio soap operas would call "coquettish."

Chip took the bait. "Oh, now, don't leave"—Esther immediately stopped and smiled—"Let's all three of us go together." Esther's face drooped.

Cassandra had enough. "I think *I'll* go," she said in disgust. She half-wished Chip would stop her too, but, at the same time, her cousin's antics were becoming too melodramatic.

Chip chuckled. "Now, girls, as much as I enjoy seeing you fight over me, there is plenty of Chip Ackerman to go around."

Cassandra's mouth dropped. Of all the arrogant things to say! It was too much. It was crazy. She didn't know a thing about this boy and neither did Esther. Yes, he was very handsome and quite amusing—and he'd be here the whole summer—but handsome or not, amusing or not, Jewish or not, kissable or not, it wasn't worth it!

Chip was changing things. Changing things between the two of them. Changing *everything* between the two of them. Couldn't Esther see that?

Chip stood. "Come on, let's go, I'd like to see this Dead Man's Gorge. Besides, why waste such a beautiful day?"

"Fine," Cassandra found herself saying in a tight voice. "Just see if you can keep up." She bolted down the hill.

Esther and Chip stayed well behind as Cassandra led them down crooked paths that wound over stony bluffs, under canopies of resin-scented cedars, and through tall grasses rippling like ocean waves. Every now and then, she looked back at the two of them, walking so close together, and felt painful stabs of jealousy.

Esther can take him! she thought to herself. I don't care at all! But…I thought he liked me. Now he seems to like her. Chip was helping Esther cross a dry, rock-strewn creek bed and Esther was practically hanging onto him. Oh, I thought he liked me.

After nearly two hours of nonstop hiking, they finally reached Dead Man's Gorge, a steep precipice in an area of sheer cliffs, gullies, and canyons. They stepped carefully through the area. It was tricky—one wrong step could send you to the bottom of a ravine.

"Whoa!" Chip cried, taking a step back from the edge of the gorge. "I'd sure hate to fall in there!"

Esther fluttered her eyelashes. "You might never come out. And then what would we do?"

Cassandra scowled. Didn't Esther realize how foolish she sounded?

But Chip winked at Esther.

Cassandra was incredulous. This boy winked at everyone—he meant nothing by it. Cassandra felt stupid for feeling special about it.

"Why's it called Dead Man's Gorge? Anyone die in there?" he asked.

A shadow fell across their faces. After a moment, Cassandra replied in a low voice, "My mother died in there. But it's always been called that."

For the first time, Cassandra saw a hint of softness in Chip's green eyes—as if he was capable of more than just jokes and winks and ego—capable of far greater feelings than he'd let on.

"I'm so sorry," he said quietly.

Cassandra looked away. The softness in his eyes had stirred something in her. As if she needed something else! "It's all right," she said a bit too quickly. "I don't even remember her." That certainly wasn't true, but she didn't want to discuss it.

"Is that why you wanted to come here?"

Cassandra stared at him. He certainly had a gift for cutting right to the heart of a matter. She hadn't considered it much before, but, yes, it was probably why she came here so often. If she had to put it into words, she'd say it was the place she heard Mama most clearly.

But to Chip, she only said, "I suppose so."

The silence grew thick, and Cassandra knew she was the one who had to slice through it.

"We should get back," she said, trying to sound light-hearted. "Dinner will be ready. I think Bubbe's making *kasha varnishkes*."

"Sounds good to me," Chip said. Whatever softness Cassandra had seen earlier was gone, replaced by his familiar swagger.

"You'll come too, right?" he asked Esther, touching her elbow. "You can't miss *kasha varnishkes*."

Cassandra frowned. She could absolutely not spend the entire summer fretting about this boy, wondering which of the two of them he liked, daydreaming about being in his arms.

Esther gave him a sweet smile. "I wish I could."

"What's the story with your hotels?" he asked all of a sudden. "How come you always meet in secret?"

Esther cleared her throat. "We don't always do that. I visit Cassandra at The Waterfalls."

"I've never seen you there."

"Well, I do," Esther insisted. "And Cassandra visits me at Schreiber's too."

"Is that a fact, sister?" Yes, the old Chip was back.

Esther lifted her chin. "If you don't believe me"—she faltered, then forced herself to sail on—"You can see for yourself. You can come to Schreiber's with Cassandra—tomorrow."

She exchanged a secret, helpless glance with Cassandra.

*   *   *   *

The sun was flanked by richly colored clouds of copper the next morning when Cassandra and Chip ventured out after a quick breakfast of pot cheese and dried figs.

Esther hadn't lied—exactly. Cassandra *had* been to Schreiber's—even if she couldn't remember the last time. Nor could Cassandra remember the last time Esther had been to The Waterfalls.

A group of children played a boisterous game of tag in the pasture while the hotel's cows crowded under an ancient oak tree on the edge of the woods, chewing serenely in unison. At the hotel, husbands played pinochle while wives played canasta at outdoor tables with striped umbrellas.

"What a beautiful morning," Chip said, stretching his arms lazily over his head in an appreciative salute.

"Yes, beautiful," Cassandra agreed, wanting to do the same, but feeling too self-conscious. The morning sunshine made the tips of Chip's hair glisten like spun gold. Cassandra admired the effect. She couldn't believe she had him all to herself. At least till they got to Schreiber's and Esther sunk her claws into him. Chip caught her admiring look and winked at her.

Cassandra grimaced. "Why do you wink so much?"

His eyes sparkled playfully. "Why do you breathe, sister? Winking is what I do. Why—does it bother you?"

"No," she admitted shyly. "I…kind of like it."

"That's why I do it."

"Because you know I like it?"

"Because I like *you*."

"You do?" she breathed. "But you wink at Esther too."

"I like her too."

"Oh," she said, feeling deflated. "So you like both of us?"

"Is there something wrong with that?"

"No," she replied quickly.

They reached the top of the hill, walked past the waterfalls, and stopped at the fence that separated the hotels.

"Now it's my turn to ask questions," Chip said.

"All right," Cassandra answered cautiously.

"Why do we have to sneak in here?"

"We're not sneaking in."

"We're not? My mistake! Why is this fence here?"

Cassandra paused. "Pop built it."

Chip nodded knowingly. "And does he know where we're going?"

"Well, no," Cassandra said. "But I don't always tell him where I go." She added defensively, "Besides, he knows Esther's my best friend. And that I go to Schreiber's sometimes."

Actually, Cassandra wasn't sure about that. Pop, of course, knew she and Esther were best friends, and that she'd been to Schreiber's. Not that she'd ever sat down and discussed it with him. Still, the reason she and Esther always met secretly was because they'd assumed it was a bad idea to flaunt their friendship in front of their fathers. It was sad, really, that they felt they needed to do that.

Chip folded his arms across his chest. "What's the story, sister?"

"What do you mean?"

"Come on, give it up, what's going on? Your fathers are brothers, but they have this huge fence, and you and Esther meet secretly. You can't fool old Chip. He's on the case."

"And who are you—Sherlock Holmes?"

"Elementary, my dear Watson," he responded in a heavily accented voice.

Cassandra laughed—she couldn't help it. "Well," she said. "Our fathers...don't get along."

"Why not?"

Cassandra thought about it. "I don't know," she said truthfully. "Something happened. A long time ago. Nobody talks about it. Bubbe won't even tell me."

"Ah, you've got to work her over," Chip replied. "We'll crack this case—don't you worry. This gumshoe gets to the bottom of all mysteries for pretty clients."

Cassandra's ears reddened. She hid a smile.

"One more question," Chip went on. "What are Esther's parents' names?"

"Uncle Max and Aunt Edith."

"Check," Chip said. "What do we do now?"

"Crawl through a hole in the fence," she answered sheepishly.

Chip nodded. "Right—as long as we're not sneaking in."

There was a frayed hole in the fence big enough for one person to fit through. Cassandra shimmied through it first, followed by Chip. They found themselves on a hilltop overlooking Schreiber's.

"Whoa!" Chip exclaimed.

Schreiber's was small in comparison with big Catskills hotels like Kutsher's, but it was grand, with white columns, a wraparound porch, and an aquamarine swimming pool. It looked like an ancient fortress the way it was nestled snugly into the lush valley below them.

"It's the Taj Mahal!" Chip said.

Cassandra shaded her eyes with her hand. "Our hotel is nice too."

Chip glanced at her in disbelief. "Please have your eyesight checked."

Cassandra frowned. "A lot of guests like...a more simple hotel. The children love the farm animals." She thought of Pop's newspaper advertisements: *We may not have a casino/We may not have a swimming pool/But we have heart/ We are the haimish place for your family.*

The Waterfalls had plenty of heart. And yet, was it right to "bury the competition," as Pop was trying to do, when it was his own brother he was trying to bury? She and Esther had grown up with their fathers' feud in the background. They were used to it. But now Chip was changing that too.

They made their way down the hill. The hotel swarmed with people getting in and out of automobiles, unloading valises and steamer trunks, trying to control packs of unruly children. Cassandra noticed instantly that these guests were better dressed than the guests at The Waterfalls. And they had cars. Most of the guests at The Waterfalls came by train. Those with money came by hired hack. But these guests were climbing out of maroon Packards, gray Buicks, tan DeSotos, dark-green Chryslers, and black Oldsmobiles. Even when guests at The Waterfalls had cars, they drove modest makes like Plymouths and Studebakers.

Chip must have noticed this too, because he murmured, "Get a load of all these snappy roadsters..."

In the middle of everything was Uncle Max. He was standing in front of the frosted-glass doors that led inside the hotel, welcoming his guests with a friendly handshake and warm smile. The resemblance was uncanny. Uncle Max looked exactly like a younger version of Pop, but there was an unmistakable weariness about him. The way his cheeks sagged and his shoulders drooped—it looked as though Uncle Max was carrying the weight of the world on his back.

Uncle Max spotted Cassandra right away. Cassandra inadvertently held her breath to see how her uncle would react to her sudden appearance, but she needn't have worried. Uncle Max's entire face brightened, as if the sun had risen across his sunken cheeks.

"Cassandra!" he cried. "My goodness, look at you! Why, you're a young lady!"

He enveloped her in a smothering hug that left her breathless. Then he held her out at arm's length and looked searchingly into her face for so long that Cassandra began to feel peculiar.

She wondered if he was seeing himself in her, or in Pop, since the three of them looked so much alike. But then she realized it was something else, and her skin prickled with goosebumps.

Uncle Max was waiting.

He was waiting for a message from his brother delivered personally by his niece. Uncle Max was waiting for Cassandra to tell him something—tell him the thing he'd been waiting to hear for years. Cassandra had no idea how she knew this, but she did. What this message might contain Cassandra did not know, but she could tell by the pure longing in Uncle Max's eyes that he wished for it with all his heart.

When she didn't say anything, Cassandra could see Uncle Max slowly accept that he was not going to receive this message. His entire posture seemed to sink several notches—it was as if he was wilting right before Cassandra's eyes.

"What brings you?" he asked, wiping clumsily at his eyes. Was her uncle holding back tears?

"I'm visiting Esther," Cassandra replied as cheerfully as she could, but it came out sounding odd. "This is Chip Ackerman. He's working at our hotel this summer."

He and Chip shook hands. Uncle Max checked his watch. "Esther's probably in the kitchen right now helping her mother," he said. When he said "mother," something painful crossed his eyes.

Cassandra began to pull away from him, but he continued to hold both of her hands tightly in his. He swallowed hard, his Adam's apple bobbing up and down in his throat. Cassandra stared at him in alarm. Was he trying to compose a message of his own for Cassandra to take back to Pop? But, his face hardened, and Cassandra knew whatever peace offering Uncle Max might have considered was gone. He let go of her.

Cassandra slowly backed away from him, resisting the impulse to run. The experience had totally drained her. She felt limp—as if she could not take another step without assistance. She was glad to have Chip beside her, because he seemed to sense this, and allowed her to lean into him as they picked their way slowly through the crowd.

Even though Schreiber's was lovely, it seemed cold to Cassandra. It didn't seem homey like The Waterfalls. There was no grassy pasture, no cows, no big red barn. Cassandra even missed the pungent odor of manure that seemed to float above The Waterfalls like a permanent cloud. Heart—that's exactly what it was missing. Schreiber's had no heart. It was too perfect—almost phony, unreal, not *haimish* at all—it was as if Schreiber's had been built in a great desperation simply to show off. Cassandra didn't know where this thought came from, but it felt as true as the sky above them.

They passed the swimming pool, which overflowed with guests in colorful swim trunks. A Philco radio nearby blasted *Zing! Went the Strings of My Heart!* above the sounds of laughter, conversation, and loud splashes of water.

They reached the hotel kitchen. Aunt Edith and Esther stood behind the shiny counter—china doll twins with their cornflower-blue eyes and black curls. In front of them were mixing bowls piled high with cookie dough. Staff in crisp uniforms fluttered about them like butterflies.

Cassandra took a deep breath and stepped forward boldly. Aunt Edith looked up, her expression registering the possibility she'd just come face to face with a ghost.

"Cassandra?" she whispered.

Cassandra did her best to smile breezily, as if it were the most natural thing in the world for her to be here.

Aunt Edith wiped her hands on her apron and walked forward tentatively. In an instant, Cassandra was smothered in another family hug.

"How is your father?" Aunt Edith asked after she'd let go. Uncle Max hadn't asked that question.

"He's well," Cassandra replied uneasily.

"And Bubbe?"

"She's well too."

"Good. I'm glad."

Cassandra introduced Chip.

"What a nice surprise!" Esther pronounced, on cue and totally unconvincingly. She turned to her mother. "Would it be all right if we had dinner now?"

"Of course, dear," Aunt Edith replied. "I'll get someone to serve you."

Esther led them into the dining room, which was set for dinner, but was empty at the moment, because it was still only after breakfast.

At The Waterfalls, the dining room was simple and modest. It was a large room, but the walls were painted a simple white, and the wood floor was scuffed and scratched in many places. Pop had stenciled a pretty border of purple hydrangeas across the top of the walls.

At Schreiber's, the dining room was ornate, with shiny silver-and-gold wallpaper, a sparkling chandelier hanging from the center of a carved, gold-leafed ceiling, thick white tablecloths, and lace-edged napkins tucked into glittering water goblets like filigreed bouquets. The floor was tiled with gleaming black-and-white squares that echoed smartly under Cassandra's shoes.

Cassandra had the feeling the rooms at Schreiber's were similarly fancy. They were probably bigger than those at The Waterfalls, and may even have had private baths and telephones.

Cassandra had never envied Esther, but she did now. Her cousin lived in a palace! And, Cassandra thought suspiciously, Esther probably had much fewer chores than she did.

The three of them sat down. But no sooner had Esther reached for the basket of bread rolls on the table than the three of them were overcome by the strong stench of smoke.

CHAPTER 7

▼

Instinctively, Cassandra, Esther, and Chip scrambled out of their seats and ran back into the kitchen. Chip got out of his chair so fast it crashed backward onto the floor.

Fire.

It sent an instant jolt of panic through Cassandra, and she thought not only of Mama, but the twelve people who died last year when Putterman's Bungalows burned to the ground.

When they entered the kitchen, though, they saw no flames, just Aunt Edith looking terrified. Uncle Max barreled into the kitchen as if he'd been shot from a cannon.

He was out of breath and his face was bright red. "Fire in the pine forest," he said between loud pants of air. "I'm rounding up able-bodied men. The ranger called an airplane."

The pine forest! Why, that was next door. If it wasn't stopped...

Uncle Max glanced at Chip. "Come with me." Then he looked at Cassandra and Esther. "We'll need you too." He said to his wife, "I'll see you there." Then he motioned for the three of them to follow him to his black Dodge.

An enormous cloud of dark smoke hovered in the distance, and the air smelled thickly of burning wood. All around them, men were jumping into automobiles and racing away. Fires were so dangerous in the Catskills that the law allowed anyone to be drafted to help fight them—even tourists from the city.

As Uncle Max's Dodge got closer to the forest, the air got darker and hotter, and Cassandra heard what sounded like great ripples of thunder. An orange airplane buzzed low across the sky. It was the Forest Service airplane that Uncle

Max had mentioned. The airplane would monitor the fire from above and radio information to the rangers on the ground.

Uncle Max stopped the car on the edge of the forest and jumped out in one swift motion. Cassandra, Esther, and Chip followed. Everything seemed chaotic. Men wearing square tanks on their backs made of tin collected rakes, axes, and shovels from the back of a big truck. Rows of buckets were lined up haphazardly by the truck. Everyone shouted and talked all at once.

Uncle Max grabbed a tank and strapped it to his back. It had a pump and hose attached to it. He bent down to the girls and said in a voice that sounded very businesslike, "You girls know where every spring and stream flow." He pointed to the rows of buckets. "Fill those buckets with water and help the men pour it into their tanks. You'll be paid 30 cents an hour." With that, he grabbed an ax and shovel in each hand and hurried toward the forest.

Cassandra and Esther beamed at each other. They were going to be paid!

"We better get started," Cassandra said, leading her cousin to the row of buckets. The girls grabbed a bucket in each hand and quickly made their way out of the area.

"Let's go to the stream by the rabbit den," Esther said as they half-ran and half-walked over the steep hill.

"No, the stream by the grove of walnut trees is closer," Cassandra replied, then started to reverse herself, not wanting to hurt Esther's feelings. But Esther piped in, "You're right—the walnut trees are closer."

They raced to the stream that flowed by a stand of walnut trees, knelt down, and filled their buckets with water. This was where they normally collected black walnuts for Bubbe's famous meringue drops. Cassandra never imagined herself here fighting a forest fire.

It was much slower-going on the way back, with a full load of two buckets of water. Cassandra was dismayed to see that some of the water sloshed out if she walked too quickly.

"The water's spilling out!" she cried.

"Mine, too!" Esther groaned.

"Should we walk more slowly?"

"But then we'll get there more slowly."

"Yes, but at least we'll have some water with us."

The buckets seemed to get heavier with each step, but the girls finally reached the fire area, which felt as hot as the inside of Bubbe's oven. There were more men now, more shouting, more chaos. Cassandra could see the fire now too, its dancing orange flames licking hungrily at the trees around it. Branches snapped and wood popped. The fire's roar was so loud it sounded like a giant motor. Cassandra's eyes stung and her lungs felt seared. She thought of Mama, helpless, choking on all these scorching fumes, alone in the middle of all this ovenlike dirty air…

When one of the men saw the girls with their full buckets, he crouched down and motioned for them to pour the water into the inlet at the top of his tank. Esther did it as best as she could, but much of the water ran down the man's neck instead.

"Oh, no," she wailed. "I'm losing the water."

"It's all right, child," the man replied gently. "We're all doing the best we can." Esther smiled bravely and poured in the other bucket. This time, she spilled less water. When she was done, the man rose to his feet and strode purposefully into the forest.

Cassandra began to wonder where Chip had gone at the same time that a man crouched down next to her to have his tank filled. She let out a surprised yelp when she realized the man *was* Chip.

He didn't look at all like the cocky boy from the city—he looked grownup and serious. When he knelt down, his pale green eyes became just level with hers. Cassandra looked into them and felt her stomach slosh more than the water in her bucket. She couldn't keep her hands from shaking as she poured the water, which ended up mostly on his shirt.

"Oh, no," she moaned, just like Esther.

But Chip winked at her, and, for some reason, it made her laugh, which had the effect of dispelling her anxiety. She tilted the other bucket into his tank, concentrating hard on getting the water into the inlet. She did a much better job.

"Abraham!" someone called, waving at Chip. "We're at the backfire!"

Chip rose to his full height, gave Cassandra a slight nod, and trudged quickly toward the forest.

Abraham?! Who in the world was Abraham?!

Cassandra and Esther both turned to watch him go. Esther had an expression of utter dreaminess on her face.

"More water, girls!" someone yelled, and both girls immediately broke out of their reveries.

When the men weren't spraying the fire with water, they were creating fire lines—chopping, digging, and raking the ground smooth. Fire lines were areas that were cleared of brush, so the fire had nowhere to spread. Of course, fire did what it wanted, and sometimes leaped clear over fire lines, and spread anyway.

One minute the fire was on one side of the forest; the next minute it had jumped over the trees to the other side. The fire warden ran around like crazy, barking orders, summoning men, shouting instructions. What a terrible job to have, Cassandra thought, feeling sorry for him. No matter how hard he seemed to try and control the fire, the fire seemed to have other plans. Fire was unpredictable—uncontrollable—it did what it pleased.

The afternoon passed in a blur as others came to help the girls. The tourists from the city were slow and clumsy with the buckets at first. But they got the hang of things after a while, and while the fire warden continued to run around trying to control the pandemonium, the girls became skilled at getting most of the water into the men's tanks instead of down their necks.

Cassandra's fingers were stiff and her legs ached. She was thirsty and hungry. She desperately wanted to lie down on a soft bed of pine needles and take a long nap. The smell of soot and ash seemed to have taken residence in her pores.

Echoes of Mama had haunted her all afternoon, and although she was too harried to dwell on it, she couldn't help thinking of Mama trapped in all this burning heat and smoke…

She wondered if Pop was fighting the fire, and whether he'd run into Uncle Max. And then she saw them both.

Discarded tanks were stretched in a long line on the ground. Pop was on one side of the line. Uncle Max was on the other side.

Just like the fence between their hotels.

And they had their backs to each other.

Just like in real life.

CHAPTER 8

▼

The fire was all anyone talked about for days. It had burned down some of the pine forest, but had not spread to any hotels, farms, or homes.

"I'm so proud of the way you helped at the fire," Pop told Cassandra. "You were brave and calm. You're growing up to be a fine young lady."

Cassandra beamed. But something troubled her.

"Did you see Uncle Max at the fire?" she asked.

Pop frowned. "I did," he said slowly.

"But you didn't speak to him."

Pop's face darkened. "These are matters for grownups, *ziskeit*."

"Why do you hate him, Pop?"

Pop blew a noisy spurt of air out of his mouth. "Run along, *ziskeit*. Enjoy the fine weather."

"But, Pop—"

"I need to attend to my guests."

Cassandra sulked as a throng of guests filed into the dining room, chatting and laughing, and took their seats for bingo. Pop instantly turned into an animated host, giving them that morning's news: "Dr. Robert Smith and William Wilson of Akron, Ohio, have started a group called Alcoholics Anonymous...The first parking meter has been built in Oklahoma City, Oklahoma...President Roosevelt has signed the National Labor Relations Act..."

Cassandra slouched out of the room. One minute she was a fine young lady—the next minute she wasn't grownup enough to discuss important matters. She headed outside.

Doves cooed in the great elm trees above her as she climbed the hill to the waterfalls. She spotted Esther sitting daintily on the edge of their boulder. Her cousin looked as though she was going to a ladies' tea party. Her hair was adorned with a satin ribbon the color of Moxie cream soda that perfectly matched the satin bow on her cream-colored dress.

Cassandra stopped in her tracks. "Esther," she said. "You're too dressed up. We're going to climb a tree today. Remember?"

Esther tossed her curls airily. "A lady always has to look her best."

"We're not ladies, Esther."

"Of course we are."

Cassandra sighed. Her cousin was changing.

Everything was changing.

Besides, she knew full well why Esther had gone to such great lengths to look pretty today, and it revolved around two words: Chip Ackerman.

"When is he coming?" Esther asked absently, picking imaginary dust off her dress.

"Soon, I imagine. He's mending fences on the pasture."

Mending fences. It made Cassandra think of Pop and Uncle Max.

"Esther, do you think our fathers will ever—"

"I've been thinking about my wedding dress," Esther interrupted. "A mountain of ruffles would be lovely, don't you think?"

Cassandra groaned. Not this again, she thought.

"And we'll have four children, two with straight blond hair and two with curly black hair, and we'll live in a penthouse on Fifth Avenue in New York City..."

"Esther, can we talk about more important things?"

"What's more important than this? Besides, you never minded before."

"Yes, but, that was earlier."

"Earlier?"

Cassandra blurted out, "Yes, earlier, before you turned into a peacock—preening and parading for *him*!"

Esther glared at Cassandra. "How dare you call me that?"

"Well, it's true," Cassandra muttered.

"You're horrible."

Cassandra sighed again. "I'm sorry, Esther, I take it back." She stared into the distance. "I just wish things weren't changing so much."

"Well, I like the way things are changing. And I like talking about him. And thinking about him. And seeing him."

"But...we never used to fight this much."

"I told you—we have to be *mature* about it. Oh, look, he's here!"

Chip materialized at the top of the hill. Cassandra was hard-pressed to change the sour expression on her face, but Esther brightened like a light bulb. "Hello!" she called cheerily.

"Greetings and salutations," Chip replied. "So, what are we doing today?"

"Well," Esther said disapprovingly, "Cassandra wants to climb a tree." The way she said that—it sounded no better than rolling in filth!

Chip clapped his hands together once. "That sounds fun."

Cassandra felt a small sense of triumph, but knew better than to show it to either of them.

Esther pouted. "Oh, pooh, I'm not good at climbing trees." She smiled at him. "Will you help me?"

"Naturally," he said. He stuck out his elbow, and Esther practically leaped off the boulder and looped her arm through his.

Cassandra slowly dragged herself off the boulder and followed the two of them down the hill. On the one hand, she wanted her cousin to be happy. And liking this exciting boy from New York City clearly made her happy. On the other hand, Cassandra's stomach flip-flopped whenever Chip was around too.

Cassandra wrestled with her feelings all the way to the end of the pasture until she was exhausted from the effort. She was so distracted she nearly stepped into a steaming cowpie. The cows were walking along the fence in a long black-and-white line, their cow bells clanging merrily. Cassandra gazed at them, but even that failed to make her feel better. The three of them finally reached the ancient oak tree on the edge of the woods.

"Who wants to go first?" Esther asked excitedly.

"You go first," Chip said. "I'll catch you if you fall."

Esther seemed utterly delighted with this chance to fall into Chip's arms. She'll probably fake it, Cassandra thought acidly. Esther hadn't lied when she said she wasn't good at climbing trees. But she'd always somehow managed. They'd only climbed the ancient oak tree a hundred times, and even though Esther always slipped a lot, she'd never needed a boy's help before.

Esther—looking ridiculous in her tea party dress—began to climb with difficulty, her body twisting clumsily. At last, she was safely perched on a knotty triangle of thick limbs high above the ground.

"Now, you," Chip said to Cassandra.

Climbing came so naturally to Cassandra that she was sitting next to her cousin in no time.

"Whoa—you're a champion climber," Chip said in awe.

Cassandra smiled in spite of herself.

Esther swung her dangling legs back and forth. "Now it's your turn," she purred.

Chip pulled himself up and joined the girls in half the time it took Cassandra.

"You're a champion climber too," Cassandra said. "Not bad for a city boy."

"What do you do in the city?" Esther asked, batting her eyelashes furiously.

"Oh, this and that," Chip answered, flashing a grin that Cassandra knew was melting her cousin's heart—and hers. How to be *mature* about this?

"Do you go to school?" Esther asked.

"Nope."

"Do you work?"

"When I can find it."

"What sort of work do you do?"

Chip leaned back against the trunk. "Well, actually, I've always liked the country. And I really like it here. I'd like to be a farmer some day."

"A farmer?"

"Sure," he said. "Fresh air, plenty of room, trees to climb."

Esther laughed nervously. "But farms are so dirty and smelly."

"Nah, it's the city that's dirty and smelly. 'The country has advantages that the city cannot duplicate.' President Roosevelt said that."

Cassandra was impressed. Besides Pop, she didn't know many people who could quote the president.

Esther changed the subject. "Is Chip your real name?"

"My real name is Abraham."

"Abraham!" they chorused knowingly.

"Chip's my nickname, because when I was small, I chipped my two front teeth on the same day."

"It must have been your baby teeth, though," Esther said shyly. "Because you have such a lovely smile now."

Cassandra winced. Esther's lovesickness was painful to witness. She didn't sound like that, did she?!

Chip grinned at her. "Nice of you to notice, Esther."

Esther turned tomato-red, but still managed to get out another question. "What do your parents do in New York?"

He seemed sad all of a sudden. "My parents are in Chicago. They had to leave to find work. They're living on Twelfth Street with all the other Jews, but I'm not sure what they're doing right now."

Cassandra thought of the men who passed through the Catskills. Chip's parents were one of those people—people who had to leave their homes to find work—people who were hit hard by the Great Depression.

"They left you all by yourself?" Esther asked.

"No, at first I was going to go with them, but we decided I'd try getting work here for the summer. And here I am."

"I'm glad you're here," Esther said sweetly.

Cassandra had to stop herself from gagging. She was having more fun than she'd expected, even though Esther's silliness was driving her crazy. She'd always loved being in a tree, and because space was so tight, Chip was squeezed right beside her. The heat from his body was distracting her to no end. He had a sprinkling of tiny freckles across the bridge of his nose that Cassandra hadn't seen before, and decided were thoroughly adorable.

"In school Mrs. Rice showed us a picture of a Hooverville," Esther went on. "Have you ever seen one of those in the city?"

Chip's face darkened. "I've *been* in one of those."

Cassandra's mouth parted in surprise. Chip was silent for a few seconds, then he said, "I came home from school one day and all our furniture was stacked on the sidewalk in front of our building. My father couldn't keep up with the rent. We were evicted."

Cassandra remembered a little girl—the daughter of one of Pop's hired men—playing a game with her doll she'd called "eviction."

"I never thought it would happen to us," Chip went on, staring into the distance. "I remember the first time I saw apple sellers—people on the street who sold apples for a nickel. And I'd always seen people sleeping under bridges and on park benches and in doorways. But I never thought…" He shook his head. "My mother refused to wait on a bread line, but we had nothing to eat."

Cassandra didn't know what to say. This was so much different than learning about the Great Depression in school. She'd seen the photographs in the newspapers that everyone else had seen. Bread lines that stretched across vast city blocks in front of soup kitchens, where people waited uncomplainingly for their only meal of the day—waited, always waited—whether it was on a bread line or in a dim employment office. Squalid shantytowns called Hoovervilles—unceremoniously named for former President Hoover—where people lived in tarpaper shacks and ate mulligan stew. The thought of Chip there…

"We thought my uncle would be able to help us," Chip continued. "He owned a department store—he was pretty well-off. But the day we went to see him, there was a sign on his Cadillac that said, '$100 Will Buy This Car. Must

Have Cash. Lost All On The Stock Market.' And my mother was worried about him, because he'd just checked into a hotel." He paused. "You know about that, right?" When they didn't answer, he said, "Haven't you heard Eddie Cantor's new routine? A hotel clerk asks a hotel guest, 'Do you want the room for sleeping or for jumping?'"

Cassandra let out a gasp. Chip said, "But he was fine. Besides, it only lasted a few weeks. My father decided they'd go to Chicago and I'd come here."

They were quiet for a few moments. Cassandra waited for someone to say something. It wasn't like Esther to stay quiet for long. But her cousin was utterly mum. So, Cassandra cleared her throat and said, "I'm sorry, Chip, about all those awful things happening to your family."

Chip held her gaze for a long time. Cassandra felt herself hypnotized. She couldn't look away, not at all, and only when he released her did she dare to blink.

"I know things will be all right in the end," he said optimistically, sounding like Pop. "Let's not dwell on it. Let's talk about happy things."

It wasn't easy at first, making the switch to lighter subjects after hearing about Chip's family, but, eventually, the three of them did. And Cassandra realized that even though she now knew a great deal about Chip's troubles, she still liked him exactly as before. No—she liked him more. And she suspected Esther did too.

After a while, Esther finally spoke, declaring, "I want to get down."

Hmmph, Cassandra thought, she's probably upset that I'm the one next to Chip.

"All right," Chip said. "I'll get down first, so I can catch you if you fall."

"I won't fall," Esther said, giggling.

Fat chance, Cassandra thought meanly.

Esther started moving downward, smacking clumsily against the knobby limbs. Cassandra heard a sudden clatter of cracking branches.

"Oh! No!" Esther cried.

There was a strange creaking sound, an exhalation of air, and then Chip's cool voice, "It's all right. I've got you."

Cassandra hurried down the tree and sprang to the ground. Chip was holding Esther in his arms. Esther had a triumphant look of pink-cheeked rapture on her face.

Cassandra narrowed her eyes at her cousin.

She was touching him. He was touching her.

But, remembering herself, Cassandra tried to make her expression as blank as possible.

Esther had seen it.

CHAPTER 9

▼

Chip set Esther gently on the ground, but Cassandra noticed with growing irritation that Esther still clung to him.

"I feel dizzy," she moaned, placing a hand to her forehead. "I hope I don't faint."

"Lean on me, Esther," Chip said. "We better get back if you're not feeling well."

Not feeling well? Esther looked positively apple-cheeked and glowing with good health! Cassandra trudged behind the two of them, feeling ignored and forgotten and insignificant, as Esther pretended to have trouble walking so Chip had to practically carry her back.

Cassandra chewed on her lip. They looked like a couple. Maybe they *were* a couple. Esther was absolutely determined to capture this boy. Esther was going to beat her to the punch.

Cassandra made a decision. If that's what happened, she would follow Esther's advice—she would be *mature*. She would not let anything interfere with her friendship with Esther, no matter what her own feelings were toward Chip.

And she wouldn't be a third wheel either.

*   *   *   *

Harry the Knish Man arrived the next morning, barreling into The Waterfalls in his noisy Ford truck. Pop came out to greet him with Cassandra right behind. Harry sold hot knishes from his truck, which was equipped with a multi-drawer warming oven. Because so many guests stayed the whole summer—and found it difficult to get into town on a regular basis—peddlers stopped by The Waterfalls to sell guests anything they might need.

Several times a week, Bubbe would shout, "The *shmatte* man is here!" This alerted guests to the arrival of the peddler who sold bathing suits, skirts, and blouses. Sometimes a peddler with a merry-go-round on the back of his truck came to give all the children rides for a nickel.

Harry got out of his truck, removed the fat cigar that was always in his mouth, and exclaimed in a gravelly voice, "Ruby, have I got a deal for you!"

Pop replied, "I'm always glad to see you, Harry, but I'm afraid we don't need any knishes at the moment."

"Ah," said Harry, waving his cigar in a half-circle. "I've brought you something else." He reached into the back of his truck and brought out four eggs. "Duck eggs," he said, gesturing to the pond. "Just think how much more beautiful your hotel will be with ducks gliding elegantly across that pond."

Cassandra could tell by Pop's expression that he was intrigued by the possibilities. Pop was always interested in anything that brought more guests to The Waterfalls. But, it bothered Cassandra now, because she realized ever since the newspaper advertisements that it had to do with Uncle Max and Schreiber's and "burying the competition."

"You've got yourself a deal," Pop said.

They settled on a price, shook hands, and Harry chugged off in his truck.

Pop looked toward the barn, where Cassandra saw Chip arranging milk cans, and whistled for him. Chip stopped what he was doing and hurried over.

"Yes, sir," he said.

"Take these duck eggs," Pop said, "and see if you can slip them among the hens."

Cassandra felt immediately sorry for Chip. He was a city boy, after all, what did he know of duck eggs and hens?

But Chip just nodded, and carefully took the eggs from Pop, and before turning to go, gave Cassandra a bright smile. Cassandra smiled back and Pop frowned. Cassandra turned away. She wanted to help Chip with the duck eggs, but knew Pop wouldn't let her. He wouldn't even let her smile at him.

"Why don't you noodle around with the children today?" Pop suggested pointedly.

Cassandra would rather noodle around with Chip, or Esther, but with Pop watching things so closely, it would have to be noodling around with the children.

Noodling around was what children did best at The Waterfalls. The total safety and community of the hotel gave city kids the kind of glorious freedom that was demanded by long, lazy summer days. She would catch up with Esther later. And, as for Chip, well, it was better to stay as far away from him as possible.

Cassandra actually enjoyed being with the children. She took them on excursions to pick wild plums, led them into the woods to see fungus and wild mushrooms, and taught them to identify hemlock, beech, and chestnut trees. She showed them how to peel bark from paper birch trees to make miniature canoes, and turn twigs and twine into bows and arrows. She took them swimming at Masten Lake, showing them how to sit motionlessly in the water as minnows nibbled their toes, and pointed out frog eggs, tadpoles, and salamanders.

Cassandra headed back to the hotel, gathered the children into the dining room, and spent the morning leading arts and crafts, helping them make bookmarks, lanyards, puppet heads, and jewelry boxes out of colored wires. When arts and crafts ended, Cassandra announced games in the pasture.

She organized the children into two Indian tribes, Lenape and Iroquois, and helped them build lean-tos out of sticks. As the children ran through the pasture whooping their heads off and throwing choke cherries at each other, Cassandra lay on the grass and made daisy chains. Some of the children had toy gangster guns with them, which seemed to defeat the whole purpose of playing Indian, but at least they were having fun.

The sky was so blue it looked like a painting. Cassandra lay back, staring up, sighing softly. A shadow crossed her face and she jumped, startled.

"Sorry. Didn't mean to scare you."

Chip. What was he doing here?

"I have some free time," he said, reading her mind.

She sat up quickly and pulled the daisy chain off her head, feeling silly.

"No, leave it," he said. "It looks good on you."

She flushed. He was smiling, his beautiful face beaming at her. Cassandra felt her hand moving to touch him and stopped immediately, horrified. Again, he read her mind.

"Want to take a walk?" he asked, getting to his feet and holding out his hand.

Cassandra swallowed, placing her hand in his. Oh, it felt so good, his warm grip in hers. He lifted her to her feet and held onto her hand for another second or two before letting it go. They started toward the pine forest.

"I thought you liked Esther," she blurted out. Oh, dear. That was a very stupid thing to say.

He seemed confused. "I like Esther," he said with a shrug.

Cassandra decided the less she said, the better. "Oh," she commented.

He seemed tense. He stopped and turned to her. "You just don't like me, do you, Cassandra?" he asked, and he looked upset about it, depressed, almost.

Cassandra gaped at him. She had no idea how to respond. When she didn't reply, he asked sadly, "Can't you give me a chance?"

"A chance?" she repeated in astonishment.

They were in the shadow of the pine forest now, far enough so that no one from the hotel could see them, but close enough that Cassandra could make out her young charges running all over the pasture.

He leaned against a tulip tree and cleared his throat noisily. "Remember when you asked me if I liked you? If I liked both of you? Well, um, I should've told you back then, but I didn't, so, well, here it is. I like you a lot, a whole lot, I've always liked you a lot, and, well, I hope you like me too."

Cassandra looked into his lovely eyes in wonder. "You…like *me*? *Me*?"

He nodded. He seemed so earnest Cassandra almost laughed. She didn't know what to say, but she didn't have to say anything, because he leaned down, her eyes closed, and he kissed her.

*　　*　　*　　*

Cassandra wound her arms around Chip's neck and kissed him back, clutching him to her, and finally, finally, let herself stroke his hair, allowing it to sift gently through her fingers. He didn't stop her, he just kept kissing her, so she did it again, and it *was* soft. It felt exactly as she'd imagined it would feel.

He was still leaning against the tree and she was leaning against him, his body warm and nice on hers. He held her so close she could smell him, and was pleasantly surprised to find that Chip smelled like everything she loved—mint and lilacs and honeysuckle.

Five minutes ago she had none of this, and now she had all of it. Riches—that's what it was—vast endless riches. Five minutes ago, she could only admire Chip's vanilla-blond hair from far away, and only imagine what it felt like, what *he* felt like. But her whole world had changed in this instant, because he was *hers* now, and, because of that, she was richer than the Queen of England.

Kissing a boy was as wonderful as Cassandra hoped it would be. And kissing Chip was absolutely magical.

Cassandra didn't want Chip's kiss to end, but, eventually, he pulled back from her. "Are you all right?" he asked, amused.

"I'm…I'm…"

"Faint?"

She nodded.

"Must be my kissing expertise," he said with a sly grin.

She smiled.

"Did you like it?" he asked and looked anxious as he waited for her answer.

"Oh, yes," she breathed, then added, "It was…my first kiss."

"It was?" He seemed surprised.

She nodded again.

"Oh," he said. "I thought you kissed lots of boys."

That didn't sound like a compliment at all and Cassandra squirmed uncomfortably.

"Oh, I'm sorry, Cassandra," he said worriedly. "I didn't mean that. What I meant was…you're so pretty I thought a lot of boys liked you."

"I'm pretty?"

He smiled. "You're beautiful."

She giggled. "You're the one who's beautiful."

He didn't respond. Instead, he bent down to kiss her neck. Cassandra felt like one of those women in Esther's radio soap operas.

Wait a minute.

Esther.

Cassandra couldn't believe she hadn't thought of Esther until this moment. Esther would be furious—no, she would be *murderous*—when she found out. And yet, it had been Esther who'd wanted them to be *mature*—to make a pact to stay best friends.

Cassandra lifted her hand and tentatively cupped his face. He turned his head and kissed the inside of her palm. Cassandra's stomach fluttered.

"I don't want to let you go," he said. "But I guess I have to. I don't think your father will be happy about this."

*   *   *   *

The following evening was Farmers' Night, something Pop had been doing long before he'd ever hired *tummlers*.

Before the *tummlers* came—before hotels in the Catskills put on fancy events like dances and comics and singing acts—simple events like Farmers' Night were all they offered. Farmers' Night was an evening hay ride and sing along, and Pop's guests adored it.

Ever since Cassandra and Chip crawled through the fence to visit Esther at her hotel, Cassandra had toyed with the idea of inviting Esther to events at The Waterfalls. She knew Esther would love Farmers' Night. But it was…complicated.

For one thing, how would Pop react? He'd never forbidden Esther to come to The Waterfalls, but he hadn't exactly encouraged it either.

And what about Chip?

He was changing things so much!

"You have to tell her," he told Cassandra right before the hay ride. "About us."

Cassandra was overcome by a profound sense of shyness. About *us*, he'd said. *Us. Us. Us.*

"Don't wait, Cassandra," he went on. "It will only make things worse."

"But she likes you," she moaned. Did he already know that? On the other hand, how could he not?

"I know," he said. "That's why you've got to tell her."

"But…what if she hates me?" she whined, wringing her hands.

"She'll hate you more if you don't tell her."

Cassandra stared into his pale green eyes. When did Chip become so *perceptive*?

He looked at her impatiently. "Do you want *me* to tell her?"

For a moment, Cassandra considered it. And yet, she knew that was ridiculous—it had to be her.

An accordion player had passed through the Catskills a day earlier and Pop had offered him the job of leading the sing along. As Cassandra, Chip, and the guests lined up next to the hotel mailbox at the end of the road, the accordion player serenaded everyone with *My Yiddishe Mama, Oifn Pripitchek*, and *Vie a Hien Zol Ich Gayn*?

The guests clapped in time to the music as they waited for Pop to bring around the hay wagon. Some took photographs of the mailbox. City people loved the rural mailboxes of the country. The hotel's ordinary, galvanized-iron mailbox was an exotic artifact that always spelled summer to them.

But Cassandra barely paid attention. She was so nervous her stomach was doing somersaults.

"It'll be all right," Chip whispered to her, squeezing her hand furtively, then dropping it immediately when the hay wagon and Esther simultaneously came into view, each approaching from opposite sides of the road.

Cassandra gasped. It was like watching two cowboys face off in a western film.

"This was a bad idea," she said in a low voice. "I should've told Pop ahead of time."

"It'll be all right," Chip said again, but his voice contained less confidence this time.

Pop and Esther both seemed to reach the area at the same time. The guests, of course, had no idea what was going on. When the hay wagon lurched to a stop, they jostled each other good-naturedly to be first on line.

Pop and Esther each froze in place. Cassandra looked from one to the other. Pop had an expression on his face she'd never seen before. What was it exactly?

Regret?

Pop usually said what was on his mind and never thought twice about it. So, Cassandra was shocked when he began to stammer, "Esther...it's...I...I...what are you...my goodness...what a...what a...pleasure." He hugged her awkwardly.

Esther cleared her throat self-consciously. "How are you, Uncle Ruby?"

"Good," Pop said, nodding, as if the two of them were having a normal conversation. "We're doing better than ever. We're so full this year we had to turn guests away."

It struck Cassandra as odd for Pop to answer Esther's question in this manner. When Esther asked Pop how he was, Cassandra was sure she'd meant it generally, in the normal way people asked that question. Esther had surely not meant to ask how well the hotel was doing, and yet, that's how Pop had answered her. It distressed Cassandra, because she feared her father was *obsessed* with having a successful hotel—no—with having a hotel that was more successful than his brother's.

Pop and Esther made uncomfortable small talk, then Pop seemed to have gotten enough discomfort out of Esther's unexpected arrival. He mumbled something about getting the hay ride started, and, with a stiff smile, walked away.

Esther turned to Chip. "Cassandra was telling me about the duck eggs," she said, her eyelashes fluttering.

Chip grinned. "Ah, yes, the famous duck eggs," he said pleasantly. "Well, it wasn't easy, and I have the bite marks to prove it, but I believe I've placed each of those eggs in a good chicken home."

Cassandra was amazed. Esther was only picking up where she'd left off with Chip, but, instead of feeling uneasy, Chip was as comfortable as could be about it.

Cassandra didn't have time to think about it, because everyone was soon aboard the hay wagon. Pop was at the tractor's helm, the accordion player was singing and playing, and Cassandra had seated herself on a prickly hay bale between Chip and Esther. It struck Cassandra as apt that he should sit between them.

Esther stood up just as the hay wagon lurched forward and lost her balance. Chip instinctively grabbed her so she wouldn't fall and Esther settled into his lap with a dreamy look on her face.

If Cassandra didn't know better, she'd think Esther planned it.

Cassandra tried very hard not to make any facial expressions she'd regret later. Esther was *not* getting up! She gritted her teeth as Chip held Esther and the wagon rolled forward.

That should be *me*, she thought in irritation, *I* should be the one in his lap.

He likes *me*!

Doesn't he?

Oh, dear.

Cassandra wanted to trust Chip, but at that moment, she couldn't.

Maybe he'd lied. Maybe it *was* Esther he really liked.

Cassandra looked away from the two of them. She concentrated on the countryside. The leaves on the trees rustled, insects sang, and the accordion played mournfully.

They passed the High Cliff House, Colner's Hilltop Lodge, Pine View Farm, and the Ben-Joseph Lakeside Inn. They rattled down a bumpy lane between fields filled with lupines and coneflowers, turned down a rutted road that opened up to a splendid view of the mountains, and rumbled past a snarled beaver dam that blocked a rushing brook overhanging with green curtains of willows. They passed bungalow colonies, a chicken farm, various hotels, and the creamery.

Cassandra breathed the sweet *luft* deeply, then let herself peek at Esther and Chip again. She instantly wished she hadn't. Esther was burrowed deeply into him. Steam rose from Cassandra's ears. She didn't know which one of them she hated more.

When the hay wagon finally returned to the hotel, Chip offered Cassandra help getting down. Cassandra angrily shrugged him off and Esther looked questioningly from her to him.

"I'm leaving," she mumbled, and even though it meant missing Bubbe's lemon pie, she ran away.

*   *   *   *

She didn't know where to go. But she ended up at the waterfalls.

Why did Chip have to come to the mountains? Why did he have to change everything?

"I thought you might be here," she heard someone say.

She looked up. It was Chip. She hadn't heard him approach at all. He sat down next to her. Cassandra turned away from him.

"Why did you leave like that?" he asked.

Because you let Esther sit in your lap? Because you're a liar? Because you're a jerk?

She shrugged. "You seemed perfectly fine without me." She hoped the edge in her voice sounded as mean as she felt.

He seemed startled. "Did I do something wrong?"

"You let her sit in your lap!" she yelled.

"Oh, Cassandra," he said, reaching for her, but she batted him away.

"If I'd acted any differently than normal, she would have suspected something," he said.

There were so many feelings spinning inside Cassandra—they felt like madly orbiting planets—that she didn't know where to begin. She grabbed one at random and said it out loud.

"I can't believe…you're really mine." There, she'd said it.

His face registered extreme surprise. "But I am yours. Can't you tell?" He grabbed her hand. "Just tell me what I can do to make you believe it and I'll do it."

Cassandra realized in that moment she was acting like a whining, demanding, silly little girl. Chip wasn't a liar or a jerk. He was right. What could he have done about Esther in his lap? Nothing. It was Cassandra's fault, really. If she'd told Esther…She was being terribly unfair to him—and he was being so sweet to her. But he was waiting for an answer. Maybe if she replied in a way that was clearly a joke…

"Well," she said, trying to make her tone light, "I think it would be helpful…if you called me Your Highness from now on."

He arched one eyebrow. "Is that so? And, should I bow too, Your Highness?" She smiled. "Oh, yes, definitely."

"Well," he said, pretending to think about it. "I guess that's pretty reasonable." He got to his feet, bowed to her with great flourish, and said, "Would it please Her Highness if her humble servant kissed her right now?"

Cassandra stifled a giggle. "Yes, Her Highness would like that."

He took her in his arms and Cassandra melted into him.

— EST. 1971 —

COMMUNITY
BOOKSTORE

PARK SLOPE, BROOKLYN

COMMUNITY BOOKSTORE

143 7TH AVENUE

BROOKLYN, NEW YORK 11215

718-783-3075

INFO@COMMUNITYBOOKSTORE.NET

COMMUNITYBOOKSTORE.NET

@COMMUNITYBKSTR

CHAPTER 10

▼

"What's your father like?" Cassandra asked.

Chip rubbed his nose against hers. They were at the waterfalls the next day.

"A lot like me," he replied, winking at her. "You'd like him."

She smiled. "Does he wink too?"

"Where do you think I learned it?"

She let out a laugh. "What sort of work did he do before…"

"He was a tailor."

She nodded. "How about your mother? What's she like?"

"You'd like her too," he said. "And she'd definitely like you."

Cassandra's cheeks turned pink. "Do you have any brothers or sisters?"

"Yup, a little brother. Five years old. Drives all the girls crazy."

She giggled. "Just like you."

"That's right," he said, laughing. "I'm teaching him to follow in my footsteps."

"Do you miss your family?"

He blinked several times. "Yes," he said quietly.

She swallowed. "Why didn't they come here with you?"

He stared into the distance. "My father didn't know if he could get a job here. All he knows how to do is be a tailor. He knows someone in Chicago who's in the business." He paused. "I just hope they're not waiting in Al Capone's bread line right now."

Cassandra let out a laugh. He wanted her to laugh—she knew that. Chip joked more than anyone she knew—it was the way he kept cheerful. He was one of the most cheerful people she'd ever met, and that was amazing, considering what he and his family had been through.

"How did I ever get you?" she breathed, mortified she'd actually uttered this question out loud.

He smiled. "You kissed me back."

"Is that all?"

"Well, you could've slapped me across the face."

"What girl would do that?" she blurted out.

"You'd be surprised."

They heard thrashing footsteps and Cassandra jumped out of Chip's arms. Esther suddenly appeared at the fence.

"What are you two doing here?" she asked, looking puzzled.

Cassandra struggled to compose her expression. But Esther didn't seem to be paying any attention. In fact, she seemed to have forgotten about Cassandra completely. She zoomed to Chip's side.

"Do you think you can get any time off today?" she asked shyly.

"I wish I could," Chip replied. "But I'm afraid I have too much work today."

"Oh, pooh, that's too bad," Esther said. She turned to Cassandra with a sad sigh. "I guess the two of us can pick raspberries."

Cassandra felt exactly the way Esther made her sound—like a second-rate substitute. "All right," she said listlessly.

She got up reluctantly. Picking raspberries with Esther was an activity Cassandra usually enjoyed. But today she wanted to spend the afternoon with Chip. This sneaking around behind her cousin's back was getting tiresome. Cassandra knew she had to tell Esther. Except the very thought terrified her.

They left Chip sitting on the boulder and made their way down the hill. Cassandra turned back twice to look at him. Each time he winked at her. It made her stiffen with fear. What if her cousin noticed? She really needed to tell Esther. But how? How to bring it up, even?

They collected straw baskets from Bubbe's kitchen and headed out to the raspberry brambles. As usual, Esther ate more than she picked.

"I wish he could come with us," Esther said as she moved along the row of bushes. "He really seems to like it up here. But I can't believe he wants to be a farmer! Can you?"

Cassandra couldn't imagine eating anything right now. Her basket was empty, her stomach tossed, and she wondered how on earth she was going to reveal her big secret to Esther when her cousin was being so chatty and carefree.

"Um, Esther—" Cassandra said, her stomach in knots.

"Maybe he can get some time off tomorrow," Esther went on. "Maybe we can come back here. I guess I should leave some raspberries for him then." She giggled.

"Um, Esther—" Cassandra said again.

"Mmmm," Esther said, closing her eyes. "That one was really sweet." She opened her eyes, looked at Cassandra, and asked, "What's the matter? You're as white as a ghost."

Cassandra gulped. Although Esther would be furious, she would be more furious if Cassandra didn't tell her. She was momentarily distracted by the sight of a monarch butterfly, its orange and black wings fluttering softly as it fed on milkweed nectar.

"Um, well…" Cassandra began, her voice failing her. She coughed. "I need to tell you something—something important."

"What?" Esther asked, her face expectant. She was still chewing on a raspberry, still enjoying its sweetness, still absorbed in thoughts of bringing Chip to this spot. She was untroubled and happy, and with Cassandra's next words, all of that would change.

Cassandra realized in that moment she couldn't do it. *She just couldn't do it.* She couldn't shatter the carefree happiness that shined so clearly on her cousin's face.

"Oh, um, well," she muttered. "It was…really brave of you to come to The Waterfalls the other day." She added truthfully, hopefully, her heart aching with the thought, "I don't want us to ever fight…like our fathers."

Esther nodded. "We'll always be best friends, Cassandra. No matter what happens with our fathers. Maybe they'll make up one day. Maybe they won't. But we'll always be best friends."

Cassandra nodded, wishing with all her might that Esther's words would ring true. When she returned to The Waterfalls, she found Chip mucking out stalls in the barn.

"Did you tell her?" he asked without missing a beat.

"No," she said, lowering her eyes guiltily.

He sighed. "I know it isn't easy, Cassandra, but you've got to tell her." He added ominously, "You're playing with fire."

Cassandra stiffened. *Fire.* "I'm going to tell her," she said, meaning it in that moment.

*   *   *   *

Cassandra and Chip snuck around all week. One evening, they sat by the pond under cover of darkness. Fireflies blinked on and off around them, their yellow-green bodies twinkling like tiny stars. Cassandra knew her father and grandmother were probably wondering about her, but she was home, after all, and she wanted to spend just a few more minutes alone with Chip.

Cassandra sat right in Chip's lap. His arms were wrapped around her, and she felt like she was in a warm, safe cocoon. He kissed her on the cheek three or four times, all in a row, and she laughed, because it tickled. And he tightened his arms around her and kissed her more, as if he knew it tickled her, until she was laughing and squirming and protesting, but he wouldn't let her go, and kept her locked in the warm, safe cocoon.

"*Druchus*! These godforsaken insects!"

Chip and Cassandra quickly untangled themselves from each other.

Bubbe, in her flowered house dress and black shoes, was coming toward them. She swatted violently at the air in front of her face and let out a long string of Yiddish curses.

Cassandra had to bite her lip to keep from laughing. Bubbe must have truly been worried about her, because nothing dragged her grandmother out of her kitchen to the pond at this time of night when every insect in the Catskills made its evening appearance. Bubbe detested bugs.

When Bubbe spotted the two of them, she grabbed her granddaughter and squeezed her to her chest. She stroked Cassandra's hair, and Cassandra noted wryly that she did not comment on its messy appearance.

"Where were you?" she scolded. "Come inside this instant. You must be famished."

Ah—food—the thing that was always foremost on Bubbe's mind.

"You, too," Bubbe said, seizing Chip by the sleeve, not seeming to care at the moment why the two of them were alone.

They obediently followed Bubbe to the hotel kitchen. "Sit," she commanded. "I have leftovers. *Ess gezunterhait*."

They sat at the table as *The Bob Hope Show* played on the radio and Bubbe piled two plates with gefilte fish, pickled tomatoes, and stewed prunes, and set them down in front of them. Cassandra wrinkled her nose in disgust and picked at the food with disinterest. It was too bad there was no brisket or peach short cake left over. These leftovers were some of the most unappealing foods on the menu.

Chip, on the other hand, polished off his plate in a matter of minutes. Cassandra felt queasy. Didn't he know Bubbe would just fill it again? As expected, when Bubbe saw his clean plate, she reloaded it. Chip polished off that one too, so she reloaded it for a third time. Cassandra swallowed back the urge to retch.

When Bubbe wasn't looking, though, he smiled at her, and that's when Cassandra realized Chip knew exactly what he was doing. Bubbe placed a hand on Chip's shoulder and beamed. "This boy has a fine appetite," she said approvingly.

Chip might have sacrificed a decent supper, but he'd just made a friend for life.

After they'd eaten, Bubbe shooed them out to their separate destinations, and it happened so quickly that Cassandra didn't even have the chance to say good night to Chip. She would see him again, of course, but she wondered for how long she'd have to keep her feelings hidden.

When daylight came, everything would be different again. There would no cover of darkness that allowed Cassandra to sit in his lap by the pond.

There would be interruptions, there would be chores, there would be Pop.

There would be Esther.

As Cassandra drifted off to sleep in her bungalow, she wondered if all the magic she'd felt tonight would be there again when she woke up.

CHAPTER 11

▼

Chip found some free time a few days later, and the three of them climbed the ancient oak tree again.

Cassandra didn't think it was possible, but Esther even fell out of it again. And Chip treated Esther exactly as he had before—he carried her, let her sit next to him, let her fall on him, let her climb all over him—Esther tried everything!

It was while they were heading back to the hotel that Esther pretended to see a rattlesnake.

"Ahhhhhh! A snake!" she screamed and climbed right on top of Chip in mock terror.

"Ahhhhhh!" Cassandra screamed in response before realizing there was no snake—that Esther was just up to her tricks again.

Chip struggled to balance Esther in his arms.

"I thought I saw a rattlesnake," Esther breathed, throwing her arms around his neck.

Chip looked at her blankly, then set her back down on the ground. Esther's expression was one of absolute and total disappointment. Cassandra hated to admit it, but her life had turned into one of Esther's radio soap operas.

The three of them were spending so much time together that even though things were topsy-turvy, good things were happening too. They were visiting each other's hotels more. Pop and Bubbe were used to seeing Esther at The Waterfalls now, and Uncle Max and Aunt Edith were used to seeing Cassandra at Schreiber's.

Eventually, they even took down a tiny portion of the fence, so that they didn't have to crawl through the frayed hole anymore. Might the whole fence come down one day at this rate? Cassandra wondered about it. Still, she knew things could not remain so rosy as long as she and Chip kept their secret.

Esther was at The Waterfalls one afternoon helping Bubbe and Cassandra prepare *challah*, the braided egg bread that was served every Shabbos. One of Bubbe's favorite shows, *Fibber McGee and Molly*, played on the radio as the three of them worked together in the kitchen. Bubbe seemed thrilled to have two girls in her kitchen instead of one, or, more commonly, none, since Cassandra stayed away as much as possible.

"So nice to have two *sheyne meydeles*," Bubbe sang out as the three of them kneaded the *challah* dough. "The way it should be. The way it should have been all along. *Farshaist?*"

Cassandra had been thinking about the fence a lot lately. Bubbe had never been forthcoming with information about it, but perhaps Cassandra hadn't tried hard enough. She waited until the radio announcer began pitching Ponds cold cream, then asked, "How long has the fence been up, Bubbe?"

To her surprise, Bubbe replied, "Eight years. Eight *meshugah* years."

Cassandra did a quick mental calculation. "So…Pop built it when I was five," she thought out loud as Esther stared at her uneasily. "That's when Mama died—when I was five." Cassandra knitted her brows together. "Does the fence have something to do with Mama dying?"

Bubbe sniffed loudly. "Tend to your kneading, *sheyne meydele*."

Cassandra paused. "It has something to do with Mama dying?"

Bubbe ignored her.

"Why won't you tell me?" Cassandra said, growing angry.

Bubbe walked to the sink. She ran the water and turned her back on them. The radio announcer talked about Maxwell House coffee. Bubbe dabbed her eyes with a wet towel. A moment later, she rejoined them. Her face was a stone mask, but she said quietly, "Yes, *sheyne medele*, that is why. That is why your *tatte* built that *meshugah* fence."

"But why?"

Bubbe glanced around furtively. "No more will you say that I never told you," she whispered fiercely. "My poor Sylvia died in a horrible, horrible fire." Her eyes welled up with tears. "And your uncle—her father—" she nodded at Esther— "was the fire warden on that horrible, horrible day."

*   *   *   *

Bubbe placed the *challah* loaves in the oven. Esther mumbled she should be getting home.

"I'll walk with you," Cassandra said automatically, and the two of them silently left the hotel and started up the hill toward the fence.

Cassandra couldn't describe it exactly, but she felt a knot of anger building inside her. Esther's father was the fire warden on the day Mama died. He was the man running around like crazy, shouting instructions, trying to control the fire. Why had he allowed her mother to die? Why hadn't he saved her?

"Your father was…in charge," Cassandra said, giving Esther a hostile look. She knew she didn't need to explain what she meant by that. She could tell by Esther's distressed expression that her cousin understood.

Esther bit her lip. "Cassandra, I—" she stammered. "I'm…so sorry."

Cassandra wanted to say more. She wanted to scream, "How could your father let my mother die?" But she didn't. She noticed Esther was in a huge rush to get home. In the blink of an eye, her cousin was through the fence and gone.

Cassandra stood around aimlessly, but the sound of rushing water failed to calm her. She returned to the kitchen. The sweet smell of *challah* hung in the air like a thick fog.

"Ah," Bubbe said cheerfully. "Now we can do the salads. We'll start with egg salad, then tuna salad, then fruit salad…"

Cassandra blurted out, "I like the fence. I'm mad at Uncle Max too." She added spitefully, "And at Esther."

Bubbe frowned. "Anger is not a good feeling, *sheyne meydele*. Forgiveness is better."

"Even when people hurt you?" Cassandra asked savagely. Her lower lip trembled, and she felt like she was going to burst into tears.

Bubbe pulled her into a massive hug. "Oh, my poor *sheyne meydele*. This is why I never told you. You and Esther—it's wonderful—the two of you. I want it never to change—no matter what your fathers think. Don't be angry with her. She did nothing wrong." She made Cassandra sit down at the table. "I have heavy sour cream with strawberries."

Cassandra made a face. Didn't her grandmother realize not everything could be solved with food? She watched Bubbe dance around her kitchen filling a bowl for her as Eddy Duchin and his Orchestra belted out *I Won't Dance* on the radio. She wished she could be that happy.

CHAPTER 12

───────────▼───────────

"I just had the grandest idea for an acting exercise!" Esther cried. "I'll pretend to be a lady in a tower, and you'll pretend to be a knight in shining armor who comes to my rescue."

Cassandra moaned. Not *another* acting exercise! All Esther seemed to want to do lately was engage in silly acting exercises with Chip—this was the fourth one in as many days. It used to be Cassandra who'd indulged Esther's dramatics, but now that Chip was around, he'd instantly become Esther's unwilling leading man.

They were lounging by the pasture and Chip gazed at Cassandra pleadingly, but Cassandra had a feeling her protests were going to fail, as usual. Nothing got in the way of Esther's acting exercises. She took her dreams of becoming an actress too seriously.

"Esther, really," Cassandra said. "I'm sure Chip's tired." She didn't know if he was tired or not, but he sure looked like he *could* be.

"But I need the practice," Esther complained. She turned to Chip. "Please?"

Chip groaned. "I don't feel like it."

"Please?" she asked again, her big blue eyes growing bigger.

"No," he said bluntly.

"Please?" she asked for the third time in a voice so sugary Cassandra wanted to gag.

He sighed heavily. "All right," he relented, throwing Cassandra a dirty look.

Cassandra swallowed. He'd never done that before. "Really, Esther, it's so babyish."

Esther placed her hands on her hips. "It's not babyish—it's art."

Cassandra frowned. It might be art, but it was also babyish.

"Esther—" she tried again.

But Esther held up her hand for silence. "Now, you kneel, right there," she told Chip.

Poor Chip—between kneeling for Esther and bowing for her—he must have felt like he was trapped in a court of royal idiots. He looked so disgusted Cassandra thought he might change his mind. But, instead, he sunk to one knee in front of Esther. Esther launched into a dramatic monologue: "Oh, brave knight, I have been locked in this lonely tower for so long. Have you come to rescue me?"

Cassandra would have burst out laughing if she weren't so troubled by Chip's apparent anger. She didn't know if her cousin was a good actress or not, but this acting exercise was the craziest yet! It was downright embarrassing—the way her cousin was behaving.

"I guess so," Chip replied flatly.

Esther giggled nervously. "You can't say, 'I guess so.' You're a knight. You have to talk like a knight." She started again. "Oh, brave knight, I have been locked in this lonely tower for so long. Have you come to rescue me?"

Chip looked so weary. "Yes, my lady," he said through clenched teeth.

Esther continued with her dramatic monologue. But Cassandra didn't find any of it funny anymore. Chip was losing patience with Esther—and with her. He made that point very obvious later that afternoon.

"If you don't tell her, Cassandra, I will," he said when the two of them were alone at the waterfalls.

"I'm going to tell her," Cassandra mumbled.

"Is that a fact? When is this glorious event taking place? The next time the moon is blue?"

She'd never heard him so frustrated. It reminded her of when she'd first met him, right here in this spot, when he was the cocky boy from the city. But so much had changed since then. Even Pop had clapped him on the back the other day and said approvingly, "You're the fastest milker in the Catskills."

"I'm not doing anymore 'acting exercises!'" he hissed. "I don't care if the next one is *Hamlet*! I'm not doing it!"

Before she could respond, he said, "Don't you see? It's just like your fathers— you're heading for disaster."

"Disaster?" Cassandra repeated. "What disaster?"

"A feud," he said. "A big, long, horrible feud."

"A feud? Between me and Esther?"

"Yes, a feud between you and Esther."

She ignored the impatience in his tone. "No," she said quietly. "That's not going to happen. We're best friends." She reached out to touch his hair, but he ducked out of her way.

"Well, if you don't tell her, you'll be best enemies."

She bit her lip. "I don't like it when you're angry with me."

His green eyes softened. "I'm not angry with you, Your Highness."

Cassandra blushed. "You don't have to keep calling me that," she muttered. "I was only joking."

"Actually, I think it's growing on me. Besides, I think you like it. *A lot.*"

Her blush deepened. She reached for his hair again, and this time, he let her run her fingers through it.

"I wish I was braver," she murmured.

"You're the bravest person I know," he replied.

CHAPTER 13

▼

"Why do you like Chip so much?"

It was already August. Cassandra still hadn't told Esther. It was as if the problem was something Cassandra could no longer control. It had unraveled somehow, spiraling dizzyingly out of her grasp. Cassandra felt frozen, locked into a kind of icy paralysis, unable to tell Esther even if she wanted to.

The two of them were at Schreiber's helping with arts and crafts. Arts and crafts at Schreiber's was much fancier than arts and crafts at The Waterfalls. Here the children used plaster of paris to mold miniature statues, threaded glass beads into bracelets, and gilded dry macaroni with gold paint for necklaces.

Esther smiled dreamily. "His eyes, his smile, his hair."

Cassandra frowned. "But he's a real person. He's more than just those things."

Esther glowered. "I know that." She studied Cassandra closely. "Why do *you* like him?"

Cassandra inhaled sharply. "I don't like him that way," she mumbled. It actually hurt to say this—to utter such an awful lie out loud—because Cassandra knew full well she liked Chip in *exactly* that way.

But Esther seemed satisfied with this response. Maybe *I'm* the better actress, Cassandra thought ruefully.

Esther sighed. "I can see our Fifth Avenue penthouse so clearly in my mind."

"But Chip doesn't like the city," Cassandra said. "He'll never live in a penthouse."

Esther smiled. "I'll change him."

Cassandra doubted it. What Esther was saying wasn't just silly, it was wrong. This wasn't something Cassandra could explain—she barely understood it her-

self. She only knew that she liked more than just Chip's eyes, smile, and hair—
she liked *him*. She liked the person he was, the sum of everything put together,
not just the way he looked.

On the other hand, when this summer came to an end, he would be gone.
Was it worth all this trouble to like him? She'd known Esther a lot longer than
she knew Chip. Esther was family. Chip wasn't.

She wondered again about the feud between Pop and Uncle Max. There had
to be more to it than what Bubbe had told them about Mama—it still didn't
explain why Pop was obsessed with beating Uncle Max's hotel.

"I can't wait to go to the Masquerade Ball," Esther said.

Cassandra nodded. "It'll be fun."

"I hope Chip can go too," Esther said in a dreamy tone.

Cassandra lowered her eyes. She wished that too. On the other hand, maybe it
was better if he didn't go.

"I'm going to try a few more things on him before the Ball," Esther said.

"A few more things?"

"Yes, you know, to see if he likes me."

"Esther, um, if he liked you, wouldn't he have already told you by now?"

Esther sighed. "Just a few more things."

Cassandra frowned. Would her cousin ever give up?

Aunt Edith came into the room, her nose wrinkling in distaste. The smells of
glue, paint, and plaster must not have agreed with her.

"Why, hello, Cassandra," she said pleasantly. "Now don't get dirty, girls." She
cocked her head to one side. "Are you sure you wouldn't rather swim? The staff
can manage arts and crafts without you."

Esther exchanged a glance with Cassandra. "Cassandra likes to help with arts
and crafts," she muttered.

That was true, and Cassandra didn't mind Aunt Edith knowing it. She smiled
at her aunt and hoped she didn't think she was a bad influence on her cousin. At
her hotel, the arts and crafts staff *was* her—and Bubbe and Bela and even Pop
sometimes.

Schreiber's had so many workers Esther never had to lift a finger to do anything! Of course, Cassandra liked getting out of her chores too—especially anything involving the kitchen—and Pop always insisted she enjoy her summers as
much as possible and not worry too much about helping. But that didn't mean
Cassandra didn't have work to do.

Besides, Cassandra didn't like the swimming pool at Schreiber's. She preferred
Masten Lake. The pool water tasted strange. What fun was it to swim inside a

giant bowl of concrete? Where were the fish and salamanders and sandy, squishy bottom?

If she and Esther weren't best friends, Esther would be a china princess stuck inside her palace all day, never climbing trees, never helping children paint macaroni, swimming in treated water, waited on hand and foot by a fleet of servants.

Uncle Max strolled into the room. He seemed thrilled to see Cassandra.

"Well, hello there," he said brightly.

Cassandra felt a rush of anger toward him, but remembered Bubbe's words about forgiveness. She forced herself to smile. Uncle Max beamed at her.

Did he honestly think they were one big happy family?

CHAPTER 14

▼

On the morning of the Masquerade Ball, Cassandra helped Bela collect big sprays of goldenrod from the pasture. As they returned to the hotel to decorate the dining room, Cassandra caught a glimpse of the fence, and couldn't hold in her feelings about Mama and the fire any longer. She wanted to ask Bela about it, but, at the same time, she was afraid of what she might learn.

"Bela, did Pop build…the fence…because he was angry with Uncle Max? About Mama? About the fire?"

Anyone else would have ignored such an explosive question, or at least showed some alarm at being asked it, but Bela never seemed alarmed about anything. He'd always treated Cassandra like a grownup, so she wasn't surprised at all when he replied, "I'm afraid so, young lady. But it started much earlier than that."

Cassandra wasn't sure she wanted to continue, but she asked, "What started earlier?"

"There may not have been a fence up before that awful day, but there was a fence *inside*," he said, tapping his chest. "Oh, you'd be surprised, young lady, how these things fester. They happen gradually, over time, the way a glacier carves the face of a valley."

Bela always spoke in riddles. Cassandra asked, "What 'things' fester?" Her heart, she realized, was racing wildly.

"Just things," he said. "Things that come up in any relationship. Things that, left unattended, get worse with time. Like a pine forest without rain. Dry, waiting to catch, like a *tinderbox*."

Cassandra shivered. She didn't fully understand Bela, and yet, a part of her understood completely. He was describing a feeling. A feeling of mistrust, the kind of mistrust that dried up good will between people over time, like a pine forest dried up without rain, until it was vulnerable to the destructive force of fire.

A *tinderbox.*

Bela said no more, and Cassandra didn't ask any more questions. She decided to lose herself in the dance preparations. And, by the time evening came, she'd managed to put most of it out of her mind.

*   *   *   *

The dining room glowed festively with soft candlelight—all the feathery goldenrod gave it the look of a secret garden—the musicians played, and Cassandra and Esther stood at the edge of the dance floor in their best dresses, watching husbands and wives glide by in a graceful waltz.

Esther's curls were twisted into shiny black ringlets, and her periwinkle-blue dress seemed to exactly match her lovely eyes. Cassandra felt plain standing next to her cousin in a too-starched white dress. Her hair was neatly braided for a change. It wasn't as fancy as Esther's—was it ever?—but at least it wasn't messy.

The ladies looked breathtakingly lovely as their silk, organza, and chiffon dresses in soft pastels of pale yellow, lavender, and rose trailed behind them in elegant trains. Their dresses were adorned with fabric flowers and bows, and they held cardboard masks festooned with feathers and glitter and mystery.

Pop had been so pleased with Chip's work all summer that he'd actually invited him to the Masquerade Ball as his guest.

"This boy has the heart of a true farmer," he'd said earlier that day, patting Chip on the shoulder. "He's no busboy."

It gave Cassandra such joy to see Pop take a liking to Chip. She hardly thought of him as a city boy anymore. It seemed like he'd always lived in the mountains.

Esther let out a dreamy sigh. "So beautiful," she murmured. "How I wish…" She stopped, sighed again, "I was one of them," she finished. Then, throwing her hands up, she said, "Oh, I give up!"

Cassandra coughed. "Give up?"

"Yes, give up," Esther replied, nodding at Chip, who was talking with Pop across the room. "I've tried *everything*! He should have been mine by now!" She shook her head. "I don't understand it. I guess he just doesn't like me. I thought for sure he'd like one of us." She shrugged. "Oh, well, I guess it's better this way. At least we don't have to fight over him."

Cassandra studied her shoes. Her cousin had just given her the perfect opening, but she *still* couldn't do it. Feelings of guilt and shame enveloped her, and at that moment, she hated herself. How could she have let so much time pass without telling Esther? She'd let Esther down. She'd let Chip down. In a way, she'd even let Mama down. After all, her mother had thought enough of her to give her a special name—a name that was supposed to play an important role in her future. But she hadn't lived up to Mama's great expectations for her. She hadn't lived up to anyone's expectations.

In an act of terrible timing, Chip chose that exact moment to start across the floor, stop in front of Cassandra, hold out his hand, and say dramatically, "May I have this dance?"

Cassandra felt her knees go to jelly. The sight of him—so handsome, so tall, dressed so nicely in borrowed clothes from Pop instead of his usual dusty overalls—took her breath away. He should have been the one with the name from Greek mythology, she thought, because he looked just like a god. After all these weeks, she still couldn't believe he was hers.

She was only slightly aware of Esther's reaction as she placed her hand in his and allowed him to lead her onto the floor. She'd dreamed of this moment, earlier in the summer, when he'd first arrived at the hotel. But once they got to the middle of the floor, she wriggled uneasily in his embrace.

"You're holding me too close," she whispered, glancing around furtively. "What will Esther think?"

"I don't care what Esther thinks," he replied.

It wasn't like him to say such things, but Cassandra couldn't blame him for feeling that way. She had to do something, though. "What will Pop think?" she asked.

Chip said nothing, but he loosened his grip. When Cassandra caught sight of Pop, though, he simply lifted his glass to her.

Then Cassandra spotted Esther. She was wearing an expression that sent a cold shudder up and down Cassandra's spine.

CHAPTER 15

▼

It had been a month since Cassandra and Chip had kissed for the first time, and Cassandra knew Chip had given up on her.

"You said you would tell Esther if I didn't," she mumbled to him one afternoon. This plan had sounded like a terrible idea at first, but the more time went by, the better it sounded.

But Chip held up his hands and said, "Oh, no, Cassandra, it's too late for that. She already suspects things. I can't tell her now. It's got to be you."

Chip was right. Cassandra could feel her cousin's growing suspicions.

They went blueberry picking one afternoon. There seemed to be an endless supply of blueberries in the mountains, and Bubbe liked to have them for her pies, cakes, bread, and jam.

"Um, here are some nice ones," Cassandra said, leading Esther to a bushy spot along a gently sloping hillside.

"Lovely," Esther said dully.

They picked in silence. Cassandra dropped a handful of berries into her pail with a soft *ping-ping-ping*.

"We can help Bubbe bake pies today if you want," Cassandra ventured.

"Whatever," Esther replied.

Cassandra frowned. Clearly, Esther was unhappy with her. The tension between them felt so thick Cassandra was sure she could carve it into pie wedges with one of Bubbe's sharp knives. Esther certainly wasn't revealing what was on her mind, but she didn't need to.

Cassandra cleared her throat and changed the subject. "Esther, what do you think our fathers are feuding about?"

She shrugged. "I have no idea."

"Do you think it was worth it?"

"What do you mean?"

"Do you think they fought over something important—something that mattered?"

"Maybe. Maybe not."

Cassandra stretched her back. "Do you want to pick blackberries after this?" she asked. One of Pop's favorite drinks was freshly picked blackberries mixed with sugar, whiskey, and seltzer water.

"I want to go home."

Cassandra tried not to let her worry show on her face. When she got back to the hotel, she ran into Pop coming out of the barn.

"And where are my blackberries?" he asked merrily.

"Um, Pop, what do you think of forgiveness?"

Pop seemed bewildered. "Forgiveness?"

"Yes," Cassandra said, feeling very silly. "Do you think forgiveness is better than anger?"

He rubbed his chin. "Of course, *ziskeit*." He gave her a puzzled look. "What is this about?"

She knew she couldn't tell him that. She wasn't brave enough. Besides, didn't he understand what she was getting at?

"Isn't it better if people forgave each other instead of being angry with each other?"

"Yes, of course, *ziskeit*," he said, looking toward the hotel. "I've got to balance the accounts. Do you want to talk later?"

She frowned. "No, that's all right."

He hesitated, then gave her a hug and walked away.

Cassandra watched him go. He didn't get it at all.

＊   ＊   ＊   ＊

Cassandra and Esther were making their way to Mr. Einhorn's farm a few days later, passing fields of Queen Anne's Lace so thick they resembled white foam.

Mr. Einhorn owned a bull, and farmers from all over the Catskills brought their cows to mate with his bull every year. Pop was going with some of his cows. Esther's parents were going to be there too, not because they owned cows, but because the annual event had become a kind of festive social call.

Cassandra's stomach was doing somersaults. There was too much to worry about—Esther, Chip, Pop and Uncle Max together in one place…Now, on top of everything, Esther seemed determined to confront Cassandra for once and for all—determined to force an answer out of her.

"I've been noticing things, Cassandra, things between you and Chip," she said—without any warning, without any warm-up.

Cassandra forced herself not to look cornered. She knew this confrontation had to come eventually, but she'd never prepared for it. She'd stupidly wished it would go away on its own. Well, now she'd really made a mess of things.

"At the hay ride," Esther went on, her blue eyes smoldering. "And that day we played Indian with the children. And…the Masquerade Ball. Chip danced with you much more than me, and he held you really tight. And the way he looked at you…"

Cassandra wondered if Esther could hear the blood roaring through her ears. She felt light-headed, and her vision blurred slightly. She didn't want to look at Esther, but she knew she had to. "I—he—Esther—" she mumbled helplessly.

"Yes?" Esther prodded, her mouth twisted into a sharp frown.

Cassandra opened her mouth, closed it, and opened it again. Nothing came out.

"Do you have something to tell me?" Esther asked coldly, her voice dripping with a thousand icicles.

Time seemed to stretch in infinite directions as Cassandra tried mightily to pull the truth out of herself. But no matter how hard she tugged, it wouldn't budge. It was too frozen, too paralyzed, too deeply buried by time and inertia and fear.

They reached the farm. Automobiles were parked in tidy rows around the hay fields, people were milling around, and tables were groaning under the weight of *mandlebrot*, tortes, *rugelach*, and noodle *kugels*.

Esther's icicle-cold question still hung above Cassandra's head like a gunpowder-grey cloud, but the noisy crowd interfered with any chance to talk to her cousin. The girls greeted neighbors, piled their plates with food, and made themselves comfortable on a patch of grass by a yard where a bull with a brass ring through his nose snorted and pawed at the ground.

Cassandra ate and alternately scanned the crowd for Chip, who was supposed to be helping Mr. Einhorn today. She spotted Pop, then she spotted Uncle Max and Aunt Edith, and finally, after several minutes of intense searching, she spotted Chip. She went through a dozen different plans for hailing him, but discarded each one for fear of further provoking Esther.

Esther shifted restlessly next to her, not bothering with the brand-new copy of *Photoplay* she'd brought with her, even though there was an article inside about her favorite actress, Katharine Hepburn. Cassandra was shoveling food into her mouth so fast that she wasn't stopping to breathe, but that still didn't make it taste like anything but sawdust.

Farmers led their cows into the bull's yard. Watching a bull mate with cows was probably an appalling thought to city people. But country folks weren't fazed. As the hour passed, the crowds began to thin. Soon Esther's parents came by to give her a ride back. Esther gave Cassandra a parting glance that spelled out exactly what she was thinking.

Cassandra gulped. She was alone now, but Esther's icy suspicions had remained behind, as real as the imprint her cousin had left on the patch of grass beside her. Cassandra stared at the spot, feeling miserable and confused, and wished for the hundredth time that she wasn't so spineless, wasn't such a coward. How could she have let things get this far? What in the world was she going to do *now*? She had to face Esther sometime, and her cousin was not going to let this matter drop. Cassandra's eyes misted with tears, but she blinked them back, and wondered what she should do, and where she should go. Pop had left a few minutes earlier, and she wished she'd left with him.

Chip sank down on the grass next to her. "Everything all right?" he asked.

Cassandra sniffled. "No," she said, relieved to see him. "Esther hates me."

"You told her?"

It was a lie, but Cassandra nodded.

Chip kissed her hand. "She'll come around. She's your best friend."

Cassandra stared down at her lap, great feelings of guilt washing over her in massive deluges.

"Come on," Chip said. "I know something that'll make you feel better." He pulled Cassandra to her feet.

Only a handful of farmers were still scattered around the yard, yapping loudly about President Roosevelt, the New Deal, the coming election, and better milk prices.

"It's those greedy financiers!" one farmer bellowed.

"Yes, the banks, it's true, it's their fault," another agreed.

"We've got a government of bankers, for bankers, by bankers."

Cassandra followed Chip past the hay fields to a large barn. A lovely mural of three white goats grazing in a field of wildflowers had been painted on the side of the barn by a fellow from the Federal Art Project. That wasn't what President

Roosevelt had intended for his WPA artists, but this fellow had apparently been greatly inspired by Mr. Einhorn's goat herd.

The works that Cassandra knew by the Federal Art Project were the posters in the post office that scolded, instructed, and informed people about everything from hygiene to safety. She remembered one that cautioned people not to mix gasoline and whiskey—Cassandra assumed, rightly—that it referred to driving a car. Another warned people to keep their teeth clean; another to protect their hands.

Chip opened the doors of the barn. It smelled of fragrant hay.

"A hayloft," Cassandra said. "I've always wanted Pop to build a hayloft."

Chip smiled. "Mr. Einhorn claims that jumping into hay cures all ills."

Cassandra giggled. "Mr. Einhorn jumps into hay?"

"That's what the man says. Here, I'll demonstrate."

He climbed a narrow ladder to the top of the loft, grabbed a thick rope that hung nearby, let out a yell like Tarzan of the Apes, and swung downward. He landed in the soft hay with a loud *poof.* Cassandra laughed.

Chip's head popped up out of the hay. "Works like a charm," he said. "You should try it."

Cassandra climbed the ladder, took hold of the rope, and jumped. The thrill of rushing air whistled past her ears as she tumbled softly into the hay. It was prickly but strangely warm.

"Well?" Chip asked.

"I want to do it again!"

They jumped a dozen more times until Cassandra felt the thrill of the rushing air had pushed out the worry and heaviness inside her. On her last jump, she aimed right for Chip, and knocked him down into the hay.

After several seconds of disorientation, he finally got up and said, "Oh, you'll pay for that."

Cassandra let out a mock scream and tried to get away, but he captured her and tickled her mercilessly.

"I bet you're sorry now," he said playfully.

Cassandra squealed with laughter and batted his arms away. "Yes! Yes! Yes!"

"You have to say it."

"I'm sorry! I'm sorry!" she gasped.

Chip smiled. "All right, I think you've suffered enough."

"I knew it!" a voice cried.

They both turned to see Esther—her hands balled into fists, her face purple with fury—stomp away so loudly that the ground shook under her feet.

CHAPTER 16

▼

The hayloft, which had been so full of Cassandra's gasping laughter only a few seconds earlier, fell utterly silent.

"I thought you told her," Chip said, finally breaking the awful silence.

The hard look on his face chilled her. "I—I didn't tell her," she said quietly. "I was lying."

Chip got to his feet. There was profound disappointment in his eyes. "Well," he said heavily. "I sure don't envy you." He ran a hand through his hair. "There's nothing I can do. This is your show now."

Cassandra wanted to say so many things—that she couldn't be more sorry, that she wished with all her heart she'd told Esther long ago, that the disappointment in his eyes was crushing her, that she'd gladly suffer hours of tickling if it took away the frustration on his face.

She got up. "I'm going to find her," she said with a resolve she didn't feel.

"Good luck," he said grimly. "You're going to need it."

Feeling lost, Cassandra started out of the barn. She wished Chip would come with her, but he was right, this was her show now. She looked back at him, but he was watching her with that expression of frustration on his face again, and she couldn't bear to see it a second time.

When she returned to The Waterfalls, the pond was alight with a million prisms of rainbows. It looked enchanted, and Cassandra wished that Chip or Esther was here to see it. But then she remembered that Chip was disappointed with her, and Esther was furious with her.

She had no idea where her cousin might have gone. On a whim, she climbed the hill to the waterfalls. Esther was there, perched on their boulder, her face blotchy and puffy.

She didn't speak when Cassandra was a feet away, and still hadn't uttered a word by the time Cassandra stopped right in front of her. But she gazed straight into Cassandra's eyes. After a few seconds, Cassandra wished Esther would look someplace else. The poison in her eyes actually made Cassandra take a step backward.

"I—I'm so sorry," Cassandra said weakly. "I wanted to tell you a long time ago, but I didn't know how. I wish—I wish you didn't have to…find out the way you did."

"You kept it from me," Esther hissed. "You did it behind my back. You let me—" she choked on her words in embarrassment as she remembered all she'd done "—when you knew all along. How could you? *How could you*? Didn't you know I'd be angrier if you *didn't* tell me?"

Cassandra hung her head. It wasn't possible for her to feel any more lowly or guilty or miserable. "Yes," she said. "I knew. But—"

Esther huffed, "There's nothing you can say to defend yourself."

Cassandra blinked back tears. "Esther, I—"

"Nothing—absolutely nothing you can say."

"Please, Esther—"

"I don't know why you're even trying."

Esther's interruptions were doing nothing to improve Cassandra's temper. "I'm sorry!" she cried, swallowing down a sob. "I'm sorry! I'm sorry! I'm sorry! How many times can I say it?" Her words tumbled out in a rush, her voice growing louder with each word, and before she knew it, she was shouting. "But you're the one who wanted us to be *mature*! You're the one who wanted us to make a pact! You're the one who said you didn't want anything to happen to our friendship! You're the one who put *him* over me! You've spent the whole summer making a fool of yourself!"

Cassandra had not meant to say those words, and she heard them as if a stranger had spoken them. Yet she knew once they were out of her mouth that they accurately described her feelings at the moment.

Esther looked horrified, as if Cassandra had just slapped her across the face.

Cassandra turned on her heel and stormed off.

*   *   *   *

"So, it didn't go well, I gather," Chip said.

"No," Cassandra said quietly.

They were at the waterfalls. It was dusk and the clicking of crickets filled the air.

Chip waited, but Cassandra said no more. "You don't like to talk about things, do you?" he finally declared.

Cassandra turned to him in surprise. "I do too!"

"No, you don't," he said firmly. "You'd rather pretend things don't exist."

"I do not!"

"Yes, you do," he said. "It runs in your family. How else do you explain the fact that your father and uncle haven't spoken in twenty years?"

Cassandra's mouth fell open. "Twenty years? How do you know it's twenty years?"

"I asked Bela," he said.

Cassandra was shocked. Bela was right when he'd said the feud started way before Pop built the fence! Why hadn't *she* asked Bela that question? How could Chip know something about her family that she didn't know?

"And how do you explain the fact that you don't know *why* they haven't spoken in twenty years?" Chip went on.

"I do so know!" she cried. "Because Mama died in the fire. Pop blames Uncle Max, because he was the fire warden that day."

"But that happened only eight years ago," Chip said gently.

Cassandra's eyes stung. She tried to keep down a sob, but another one waited right behind it, and that one came out before she could stop it, followed closely by another one.

Chip wrapped his arms around her. "Sometimes," he said wryly, "I think I should've gotten a job at a different hotel. If I'd never come here, I wouldn't have messed up things between you and Esther. On the other hand, you would have been completely deprived of my charm and good looks."

Cassandra snorted a laugh between her sobs, and her nose ran all over his shirt. She sniffed delicately and asked, "What do you think I should do?"

The playfulness left his eyes. "I'd hate for you and Esther to stop speaking for twenty years. Don't you see? Your father and uncle probably had a falling out— like you and Esther did—but instead of making up, they stopped speaking, and it got worse and worse, until it just, I don't know, got a life of its own, I guess. And

I have a feeling they fought over something really stupid. Probably don't even remember what it was about anymore."

Festered, Cassandra thought, like Bela had told her. *Things that come up in any relationship. Things that, left unattended, get worse with time.*

"Then the fire came," Chip continued. "And that was the last straw, and your father built the fence."

Like a pine forest without rain. Dry, waiting to catch, like a tinderbox.

Cassandra stared at Chip through watery eyes. He'd been here for exactly one summer—and had figured out what had taken her fifteen years to know—and she still didn't know it all.

He caught her stare and said, "Ah, I see that you're impressed with my excellent detective skills." He switched to an accented voice, "I told you Sherlock Holmes was on the case."

She snorted another laugh into his shirt, hoping he didn't mind the mess she was making of it.

His eyes got serious. "Don't let this feud get passed down, Cassandra." He wiped away her tears. "I know what you need. An extra-long kiss." He winked. "It's one of the specialties of the house. Would you like to try one?"

Cassandra sniffled and nodded.

He gave her a slow, sweet kiss, then asked afterward, "How was that?"

Cassandra was breathless. "Can you do it again?"

He grinned. "Whatever you say, Your Highness."

CHAPTER 17

▼

Cottony amber clouds crisscrossed the sky in an intricate show of shadow and light as Cassandra made her way to the barn, where Chip and Pop were milking side by side like two mirror images.

Pop no longer minded if Cassandra helped milk. Cassandra suspected it was because Pop liked Chip—and didn't mind if Cassandra did too. Cassandra wasn't sure if Pop knew everything about her and Chip—she didn't think so—but even if he were to find out, Cassandra liked to think he still wouldn't mind.

"Good morning," she said with a lightness she did not feel.

"Morning, *ziskeit*," Pop replied cheerfully.

"Greetings and salutations," Chip said, winking at her.

Cassandra smiled at him. She remembered the first time he'd winked at her in the barn, and how her stomach had flip-flopped. Now it just gave her a great sense of comfort.

The three of them worked in companionable silence. Cassandra couldn't think of any better way to start the day. Milking had always had a relaxing effect on her, and on Pop, which explained why Pop continued to milk when he could have easily hired men to do it for him, especially when he was needed at the hotel during the summer for so many other things.

Pop seemed to be in an excellent mood. His milking fedora was tilted jauntily to one side of his head, and every so often he burst into the middle of a Bing Crosby tune, singing so off-key that Cassandra winced and Chip tried hard not to laugh.

Cassandra wasn't so relaxed, though, that she'd stopped thinking about all the awful things that were on her mind. After a few minutes, Chip left the barn to take care of other chores. Cassandra and Pop were alone, and though she hadn't planned it, Pop seemed to be in such a good mood that Cassandra felt like she could ask him anything.

She took a deep breath of the hay-scented air and waited until Pop was done with his rendition of *Let Me Call You Sweetheart*. When he'd finished making a mess of poor Mr. Crosby's song, she asked, "Pop, is it true that you built the fence because Mama died in the fire?" A year ago, she could have never imagined asking her father that question. She held her breath, afraid to make a single noise, while she waited for Pop's answer.

But Pop neither looked at her nor responded, though she noticed that he worked more quickly.

"Pop?" Cassandra pressed, another thing she would have never done before.

"He killed her," Pop mumbled in a voice so low Cassandra wasn't sure she'd heard him right.

"He...killed her?" she asked incredulously.

Pop's eyes flashed with something frightening, and Cassandra flinched. He said icily, "She died in a fire at the bottom of Dead Man's Gorge, with no one to save her, no one to help her, not even my own brother, and it was his responsibility, he was the fire warden that day, he should have saved her. *He killed her.*"

Cassandra blinked back tears. Pop was making it sound as if Uncle Max was a murderer. Cassandra couldn't believe that. She knew nothing about what happened that day, but she knew that fire was unpredictable, that it did what it wanted, that it caused confusion and chaos and danger. She remembered the stinging heat and smoke, the sound of wood popping, the great ripples of thunder.

Uncle Max hadn't killed Mama. The fire had killed Mama.

Chip chose that exact moment to return to the barn, and Cassandra didn't know if his timing was good or terrible. He gave her a bright smile, but sensed immediately that things were dreadfully wrong. His presence seemed to distract Pop from Cassandra's awful question, though, and the three of them milked silently until they were finished, each of them grateful to have something to do with their hands.

After milking, Pop went off to the hotel, and Cassandra remained in the barn as Chip cleaned up. She hated following him around when he had chores to do, but she had to tell him about Pop. She wished he'd put down his pitchfork, hold her, and make everything go away. Why did he always have so much work to do?

But even though Chip did put down his pitchfork, and pulled Cassandra onto his lap, he couldn't make it go away, even if he wanted to. Cassandra burrowed deeply into him. Why did it seem like her nose was constantly running on his shirt?

"Why do you have so much work to do?" she asked. "Why can't we climb the oak tree now and sit in it all day?"

Chip smiled. "If I didn't have so work much to do, I wouldn't be here. And if I wasn't here, who would sacrifice endless amounts of shirts to your nose?"

Her laugh came out as a hiccup. He could always make her laugh, even when she was crying. "I wish I'd never asked Pop about Mama," she said.

"No, you were brave to ask," he said.

"But—I don't know how he could think such a thing—it scared me."

"It would have scared me too," he said. "I guess when you're feuding with someone, you think the worst things about them. Your uncle didn't kill your mother. It was an accident—a tragedy. Forget what your father said. He isn't right. He probably knows that—deep inside."

Cassandra gave him a pleading look. "Do you have a lot of work today?"

"Yes, I do, Cassandra," he said gently. "But you wouldn't be giving me a second thought if Esther was around."

"I would too."

"Come on, Cassandra, let's face it, you're bored out of your mind."

Cassandra hiccuped again. "But Esther hates me."

"Maybe, but you've got to make up with her." He paused. "You don't want this happening to *you*."

He was right, and Cassandra knew it. Besides, she was keeping him from his work, and he had so much to do. Cassandra headed back to the hotel. In the dining room, Pop was reading the news to his guests.

"Last night, at midnight, I got WNBC in New Britain, Connecticut, on the radio dial," he recited in a shaky voice. "And here's the news. President Roosevelt signed the Social Security Act…Will Rogers died in an airplane crash in Barrow, Alaska…"

The guests gasped at the news of Will Rogers' sudden death. Will Rogers was one of Pop's favorite entertainers—an Oklahoma cowboy, philosopher, film star, and writer—all rolled up into one person. He was only 55.

But, even though this news was shocking, Cassandra noticed that Pop failed to deliver it with his usual flourish. Pop's shaky voice and lack of enthusiasm couldn't be due to bad news—he'd delivered bad news before. No, Pop was affected by the conversation in the barn far more than Cassandra realized.

Cassandra knew what she had to do. She headed back outside and climbed the hill to the waterfalls. Her heart felt so heavy it actually weighed down her steps, and her head seemed so stuffed with runny nose and never-ending tears it felt like it was on lopsided.

She reached the tiny cut portion of the fence and stopped to gaze at it. What on earth made her think this fence would come down? Things seemed worse than ever. And she remembered Bela's words.

There was a fence inside.

She shook her head and forced herself forward.

Schreiber's was swarming, as usual, with people. At the pool, *I'm in the Mood for Love* played on the radio and men played water polo. Cassandra wondered how people could be so cheerful and happy when she felt so low and miserable. She wandered through the hotel aimlessly, feeling more and more forlorn, until she ran unexpectedly into Uncle Max in a narrow hall off the main lobby. He didn't seem exactly unhappy to see her, but he didn't seem overjoyed either.

"I need to talk to Esther," she said, getting right to the point.

His face was so sorrowful. "I'm sorry, Cassandra, I don't know where she is at the moment."

Something about the way he said it made Cassandra pause. "Yes, you do, Uncle Max," she said, lifting her chin and daring him to disagree with her. "You know exactly where she is, and you and Aunt Edith knew where she was when I asked the other day too. You just won't tell me."

Uncle Max averted his eyes.

"Esther asked you to tell me that, didn't she?" Cassandra went on. "So she won't have to talk to me."

He didn't answer, but Cassandra could tell from his expression that she was right.

"I'm sorry, Cassandra," he finally said, spreading his arms helplessly. He started to go.

Cassandra instinctively grabbed his shirt. "What happened between you and Pop?" she blurted out.

"What?" he asked, thunderstruck.

The questions came fast, like bullets, one right after the other.

"Why haven't you spoken in twenty years?"

"Why is Pop always trying to beat you?"

"Why is he so obsessed with having a more successful hotel than you?"

Uncle Max stared at her in astonishment. "I've got to go, Cassandra," he said softly.

"No," Cassandra said firmly, with a ferocity that surprised her. "You're not going. Not until you tell me everything, Uncle Max."

No one spoke for several seconds. Cassandra realized that Uncle Max's shirt was balled up so tightly in her fist that she was ruining it. Why was she constantly destroying other people's shirts?

Uncle Max gave Cassandra a long look filled with anguish. "Cassandra, I—"

"Tell me!" Cassandra cried fiercely. "I'm not letting you go until you do!"

Uncle Max gazed down at his feet. When he finally lifted his head, he looked so weary that Cassandra thought he might crumple to the ground in front of her.

"All right, Cassandra," he said. "You win. I'll tell you. But let's go to my office." He looked down at her hand. "You can let go now. I promise I won't run away."

Cassandra forced her fingers to unclamp his shirt and followed him down the hall to an office with a bank of large windows that let in the morning sunshine. Cassandra studied the surroundings carefully. Even the offices at Schreiber's were perfect.

Uncle Max sat in a chair. Cassandra sat opposite him.

He sighed. "All right. You asked. Here it is. Ruby and I grew up at The Waterfalls. It was our parents' farm."

Cassandra nodded. This part she already knew.

"We talked about turning it into a boardinghouse. Other farmers were doing that to make extra money. But we disagreed over everything. We argued constantly. We just couldn't agree how to run it."

Uncle Max's face hardened. "Then, one day, we had a tremendous fight." He stared at something beyond Cassandra. "Gosh—I can't even remember what it was about." He fell silent, his face contorted into concentration. "No, I just can't recall it. Ironic—that I can't remember what we fought about. Ironic—because that was the last time we spoke."

Cassandra felt her insides turn to ice.

Uncle Max went on, "We stopped speaking after that. And then, I bought the land here, built Schreiber's, and, well, here we are."

A thick silence settled between them.

Cassandra was stunned. "*That's it*?!" she screamed. "That's why you haven't spoken in twenty years?! That's why Pop is obsessed with beating you?! That's why Pop built the fence…and thinks you killed Mama?!" Her voice broke, and she covered her face with her hands.

Uncle Max was at her side immediately. "I know how it must seem to you, Cassandra," he said. "It seems that way to me too—it's something I think about every day." His eyes glistened. "I wish I could turn back time—I wish with all my heart that I could change the day your mother died. I know Ruby thinks that about me. He told me so on that awful day."

He seemed so controlled when he talked about it, yet Cassandra noticed that his lip trembled.

"It's impossible to explain—these twenty years," he said, shaking his head. "I'm ashamed to admit this, but the reason I built Schreiber's next door was out of spite. I was so foolish. When you came to see me that first day, I thought you were coming to tell me that your father was ready to mend fences. I've been waiting for that message—all these years."

Cassandra sniffled. She'd been right about that.

"It's a kind of paralysis," he went on, more to himself than to her. "Everything stops. Everything freezes. It takes an awful lot to budge it. I must have thought of going to see your father a million times, but I just couldn't do it."

Cassandra stared down at her hands. Uncle Max was hitting too close—much too close.

*   *   *   *

Cassandra threw herself into happenings at the hotel.

She helped Bubbe in the kitchen, hollowing out watermelon for fruit boats to the tune of *East of the Sun and West of the Moon* on the radio.

She molded chopped liver into tiny chicken sculptures that Bela placed at each table setting on Shabbos.

She formed a massively efficient potato, cheese, cherry, blueberry, and prune blintz assembly line with Bubbe and Bela. Cassandra cracked eggs, Bubbe beat them, and Bela mixed in the other ingredients for the crepe batter. When the batter was ready, the assembly line moved to the stove, where Bubbe ladled the batter into her heavy pan, shook it three times, *flick*, *flip*, and slid it to Cassandra. Cassandra spooned a gob of filling in the center of each crepe. Bela folded the crepe shell over the filling, fold, fold, fold, then, *tuck*, *flip*, and *pat*.

It was tedious, never-ending work, but it had the effect of settling Cassandra's mind into an organized, reassuring nothingness.

"To what do I owe this wonderful helpfulness?" Bubbe asked.

Cassandra realized she was keeping so many secrets from so many people that she could barely keep track of them all. She couldn't tell Bubbe that Chip was too busy to spend time with her, because Bubbe might wonder about that. She couldn't tell Bubbe about Esther hating her, because, except for Chip, she hadn't told anyone that.

"I just like it," she muttered. She was sure her grandmother would see clear through this pathetic lie, but, to her surprise, Bubbe beamed.

"I like it too, *sheyne meydele*," she said, and started telling Cassandra about the rudiments of *garmigiere*, the art of food presentation.

It wasn't that Cassandra didn't like spending time with her grandmother. Of course she did. She just hated working in the kitchen. She'd always hated it. So it struck Cassandra as odd that Bubbe would believe her so readily.

On the other hand, Cassandra couldn't help noticing that lots of people believed what was simply easy to believe. Pop believed President Roosevelt's New Deal would work, even though that was far from certain. And he believed Uncle Max killed Mama, even though that was crazy.

Uncle Max believed it was better to stay inside a frozen paralysis for twenty years than do anything to change it. And hadn't Cassandra believed that not telling Esther about her and Chip would somehow take care of itself?

She was more wrong than anyone.

The duck eggs had hatched some days earlier, and Cassandra spent many hours watching the four ducklings explore their new surroundings. Chip had done a wonderful job of tricking the hens into believing the ducklings were theirs. He did have the heart of a "true farmer," as Pop had said.

Something hilarious happened to the ducklings that week. The hens and ducklings went for a stroll, and, as soon as they got close to the pond, the ducklings made a break for the water. The hens raised a panicked clucking, but it was no use. Instinct won.

Cassandra laughed and laughed, then realized she'd been the only one who'd seen it. A profound sense of loneliness washed over her.

Esther would have loved it.

She'll hate you more if you don't tell her.

Chip had been so right.

Cassandra thought of Pop and Uncle Max not speaking for twenty years, because of a stupid fight her uncle could no longer even remember. She'd assumed when two men didn't speak for twenty years, it was for a good reason. She'd assumed something astronomical had happened between them. She'd told Chip as much—that the feud had started because of something that had happened in the past—but that *something* turned out to be a big fat *nothing*.

Chip had been right about that too.

Cassandra watched Pop give his guests the morning news ("The three-year war between Bolivia and Paraguay has ended...An earthquake in Quetta, India, has killed 50,000 people...") but it sounded like so much background noise.

"In Berlin, Heinrich Himmler has established the Society for Research into the Spiritual Roots of Germany's Ancestral Heritage, a breeding program to produce an Aryan race…"

Cassandra knew from the reaction of every guest in the dining room that this was very bad news. But she went outside to visit the ducklings.

Summer was coming to a close, and Pop had arranged a lavish line-up of entertainment to mark the end of the season. Tonight, there would be a magician, hypnotist, and mock wedding. It was unusual for so modest a hotel to host such extravagant shows, but Cassandra knew exactly why now.

The guests hushed that evening as the emcee introduced the magician, who stepped out in a cloud of white smoke and launched three grey-white doves into the air. He made red scarves turn into blue scarves, poured a pitcher of water into his fist, and turned an egg into an orange. He ripped up money that became whole again, guessed people's ages, and, in a grand finale, pulled a white rabbit out of his hat.

Cassandra applauded heartily, but only one thought filled her mind:

Esther would have loved it.

The hypnotist came next, declaring he could hypnotize any member of the audience into believing they were a rooster. A tall man who looked as though he'd rather be anywhere but in this room came forward. The hypnotist uttered a series of strange chants, spun the man around, and snapped his fingers, and the man immediately began to prance around the room, crowing and cackling like someone gone mad. It was so stunning that nobody spoke, but after the choked silence had passed, everyone erupted into laughter. Cassandra couldn't help joining in, for it was truly hilarious to see a grown man strut around the room like a proud rooster, arms folded back like wings lying flat, legs lifted in a comical swaggering gait.

And then it was time for the mock wedding. Every year, Pop chose the smallest female guest to play the groom, and the burliest male guest to play the bride. The guests nearly tore open their sides with laughter at the sight of a giant hairy man stuffed into a frilly white gown holding a spray of white roses under the *chuppah* next to a tiny woman dressed in formal grey pinstripes.

But Cassandra could only think of one thing:

Esther would have loved it.

After the show ended, Bela served coffee and banana pound cake, and everyone mingled and socialized, including Bubbe, who was dressed in her very best, and making a rare appearance outside the kitchen.

She handed Cassandra a glass of milk and plate that contained a thick slice of cake, then elbowed her in the ribs, and said, "How lucky you'd be, *sheyne mey-dele*, if you made a match like that." She nodded at Chip, who was on the other side of the room. "What a *mensch*. And, oh, such a Greek god! What a catch he would be, eh?"

Cassandra blushed right down to her toes. Oh—if her grandmother only knew! It seemed almost a shame to keep it a secret from her.

"But where is your twin?" Bubbe asked. "Why do I not have my two helpers anymore?"

"We had a big fight," Cassandra said glumly.

"*Vai is mir*," Bubbe said, shaking her head. "What a terrible *shanda*. Just like your fathers."

Cassandra stared at Bubbe for a long time. It was true. She had allowed a fence to go up between her and her cousin—a fence that was no different from the one that Pop had built between him and his brother. And if Cassandra couldn't tear down the fence outside, she could at least tear down the fence inside.

"No," she said firmly, "*not* like our fathers."

And in that split-second, Cassandra realized why Mama had named her after a mythical Greek legend. Mama had known—or hoped—that Cassandra would discover why her father and uncle hadn't spoken in twenty years. And Mama had hoped Cassandra would do something about it. Like the mythical Cassandra, who'd foretold only truth.

But Mama also knew that it wouldn't be easy for Cassandra. That Pop and Uncle Max would not make it easy. Like the mythical Cassandra, who was destined never to be believed.

Did Mama know the stupid twenty-year feud was over nothing. *Nothing*?! Were most feuds over nothing? Was Cassandra's feud with Esther over nothing?

Cassandra drew herself up. Tomorrow, she'd go to the place where she could hear Mama the most clearly. She would hike to Dead Man's Gorge. And Mama would show her what to do.

CHAPTER 18

▼

The sky was the color of milk. Rain spattered against the ground in a half-hearted way, then the sun put in a feeble appearance before white clouds filled the sky once more. A mass of darker clouds thundered menacingly in the distance.

As usual, Chip was busy, but Cassandra wanted to tell him at least where she was going, though she wasn't sure if she should tell him why.

"Dead Man's Gorge?! *Today*?! But there's a storm coming."

"Yes, but...I have to go today."

"Why? Why today?"

She hesitated. Should she tell him? No, she decided against it. "I just do," she said softly.

He leaned on his shovel. He couldn't argue, she knew, with the determination in her eyes, so he dangled a juicy carrot in front of her instead.

"If you wait until the next time the weather is nice, I'll go with you," he said.

It was a tempting offer and Cassandra had to think about it. Chip had been so busy lately she probably hadn't seen him for more than ten minutes a day. She didn't know how he'd manage to get so much time off to go to Dead Man's Gorge with her, but if he said he would do it, he would do it. He never broke his promises. Still, she decided no.

"I have to go now," she said.

He glanced at the sky outside the doors of the barn. "Cassandra, it's going to storm any minute. That's not a good place to hike in bad weather."

"I'll be fine," she said. "I know it like the back of my hand." Both of them knew that was true.

He sighed. "Cassandra, why are you being as stubborn as a mule? Can't you go on another day?"

She frowned. She *was* being as stubborn as a mule, but she had her reasons.

"Is there anything I can do to stop you?"

She thought he was kidding, but he wasn't. She pretended to think about it, but couldn't come up with anything. She supposed he could hold her back from leaving—he was certainly stronger than her—and Cassandra wouldn't mind at all being trapped in his arms for an entire day. But she knew he didn't have that kind of time to spare. He could pin her down and tickle her, like he'd done before, but he couldn't do that forever either. Cassandra found it intriguing—these possibilities. She'd never considered it before. The truth was—Chip had no control over her at all. He was stronger—but that was completely useless in this situation—maybe in any situation.

He must have come to the same conclusion, because he said, "Well, I guess there isn't a whole lot I can do, but there is one thing…"

He got down on both of his knees in front of her and clasped his hands together. "I beg you, Cassandra, please do not go to Dead Man's Gorge today."

Cassandra stared at him uncomfortably. She knew he was trying to be light-hearted, but there was real pleading in his eyes. He'd been right about so much this summer too—it was as if he had a sixth sense about things. The fact that he would go to such lengths now—actually *beg* her not to go to Dead Man's Gorge—gave her the chills. What did he know? She felt herself tilting rapidly toward his wishes—but forced herself to resist it.

"I really do have to go," she said quietly.

He waited a moment, then got up. "I know I almost had you there."

"Why are you so against me going?"

He gave her a funny look. "You don't know? After I just humiliated myself? Because I'm worried about you. Because I'm crazy about you. Can't you tell?"

"But…but…you're a god." For goodness sake! Had she just said that *out loud*?

He grinned. "Am I? Well, I'm glad you told me, that's good to know. Gods like it when their goddesses listen to them, though." He picked up his shovel. "I guess I can pull some strings for you on Mount Olympus. Maybe they'll change the weather for you."

Cassandra hesitated. "Why do you like me so much?" she asked, feeling her face flame immediately.

He stopped what he was doing and stared at her. Before he could answer, though, she added, "And how come you liked me…and not Esther?"

He leaned on his shovel. "Well," he said slowly. "I'm not sure how this is going to sound, but I liked you because I knew you liked *me*."

"What? But Esther liked you too."

He shook his head. "No, Esther liked the *idea* of me." He cocked his head to one side. "Don't mean to sound like a *god*, Cassandra, but this is something I'm used to. All the girls in the city follow me around too."

Cassandra's mouth fell open.

"But they don't really like me—the *real* me." He switched to a high voice. "Oh, he's so tall, he has such beautiful eyes, I love his hair, and, oh, those cute little freckles on his nose!"

Cassandra's mouth fell further open.

"Those things aren't *me* at all," he continued. "And you knew that—I could tell—you were different. I just had to figure out how to get you to stop hating me." He paused. "Anything else you want to know? Shoe size? Favorite color?"

"I do like you—the *real* you," Cassandra mumbled.

"I know. And—if you don't leave now—I'm going to hold you down and tickle you until you promise you won't go."

Cassandra hesitated, feeling shy all of a sudden. "Can I give you a kiss before I go?"

He threw his shovel aside and opened his arms. "You *better* give me a kiss before you go."

Cassandra smiled. She loved that about him—his big dramatic gestures always made her feel wonderful. She flew into him and he lifted her up and twirled her around just like those men and women did on Esther's radio soap operas.

"Did a girl ever really slap you across the face?" she asked him.

"No," he said, laughing. "Do you want to be the first? I'll give you a clear shot."

"No!" she cried, but he was joking as usual.

"You joke a lot," she said.

"Sometimes you have to joke a lot."

"I like it," she said shyly.

He smiled. "Then I'll keep doing it."

*   *   *   *

Cassandra broke into a run, not caring if the sky opened up, and headed toward Dead Man's Gorge. Her whole body tingled with happiness, except when she thought about how much Chip didn't want her to go today. But she *had* to go today. How could she explain that to him? She couldn't. She hadn't even tried.

The sky got darker and darker as Cassandra made her way quickly over the crooked paths to the sheer canyons and cliffs of Dead Man's Gorge. She was almost there when Chip's prediction came true, and rain began to fall in sheets so thick it was as if grey curtains had been pulled across Cassandra's eyes. Still, she pushed forward. Mama would help her. Mama would show her what to do.

It was getting harder to see, but Cassandra kept going. Not much longer. Soon she would be there, and Mama would be there too.

She tripped violently and let out a cry—mostly in pain but also in surprise—and sank downward, heard a loud and disturbing *snap*, and tumbled head over heels, out of control, her vision turning over and over and over, slashes of pain tearing at her skin as she fell endlessly downward, and then all was dark.

All she could think about before she lost consciousness was that Chip was right, and she hadn't listened to him. Something terrible had happened, and even Mama couldn't help her now. Had Mama tricked her?

CHAPTER 19

▼

Cassandra opened her eyes and was instantly aware of a razor-sharp pain in her leg.

She blinked several times.

Where was she?

Which way was up?

She forced herself to think. Her head felt dangerously light.

She was crumpled into a heap. Her left knee was pinned awkwardly to her chest—and her right leg—where was her right leg?

Where was she?!

She tried to shift position. But a hundred of Bubbe's sharpest knives sliced through her. She turned her head slowly, groaning at the pain it caused, and peered down at her right leg. It was twisted into a position so grotesque that Cassandra actually gasped. Then she felt something drip wet and warm and slimy, and resisted the urge to panic.

She had fallen. She remembered that much. It had started to rain, and she'd tripped, and she'd fallen. She'd pitched downward endlessly, tumbled over and over and over, sunk down and down and down.

A horrible sense of understanding finally dawned on her. She must have fallen into one of the ravines. She was at the bottom of a ravine. If it hadn't rained so hard, she would have never tripped, or fallen, or even stepped in the wrong place.

She looked upward, moaning at the shooting daggers of pain, and saw a feeble grey light. Yes, that had to be it. That was the top, and…she was at the bottom.

I'm trapped, she thought. I'm trapped at the bottom of a ravine.

Like Mama.

Cassandra peered upward again. It hurt so much she felt tears gather at the corners of her eyes. The grey light wasn't that far off, though, which meant the ravine couldn't be too deep. She was sure she could climb out—it was probably steep—but she was a champion climber. Chip had said so. But she could hardly move her head, let alone her legs. Especially her right leg...

Chip. He knew where she'd be. She'd told him where she was going. Would he come? Would he try and find her? How long would she have to stay here, in horrible pain, with her leg throbbing in agony, before he came?

Before anyone came?

She felt sleepy. She willed herself to stay awake, but the effort was too great—her eyelids felt heavier than bricks.

Cassandra shut her eyes.

Her vision went dark.

       *   *   *   *

Cassandra opened her eyes. Her head was swimming with darkness and pain and fog, but she had heard something. She felt damp and chilled to the bone.

How long had she slept? It seemed like hours.

Cassandra listened with as much concentration as she could muster. Funny—she'd never considered listening to be something that required so much work.

"Cassandra!"

"Cassandra!"

"Cassandra!"

Someone was shouting her name. Someone was nearby! Someone had found her!

She would have to yell back. She would have to summon every cell in her body to unite for that one purpose: to yell back. It would take everything she had, but she had to do it. She marshaled all the strength she had, opened her mouth, and shouted,

"H—E—L—P!"

It took so much out of her that she fainted immediately.

She didn't know for how long she was out, but when she woke, it was to the sounds of loud thrashing and curses.

Someone was here—right above her—someone had heard her! Cassandra wanted to tell the cursing voice exactly where she was, beg the voice to stay with her, guide the voice right to where she lay, but she had no strength left. All she could produce was a long gurgle that sounded like the noise an animal might make.

The thrashing and curses stopped. "Was that you, Cassandra? Did you make that sound? Can you talk? I heard you yell before. Say something! Are you hurt?" The voice waited, but Cassandra didn't reply—she couldn't reply. "Why didn't you listen to me? *What are we going to do*? You picked a fine place to fall! I can't get through here!" The voice sounded like it was on the edge of panic.

Don't leave me, Cassandra thought.

"Someone small," the voice said, calmer now. "Someone small could wriggle through all this."

The voice paused.

"Cassandra, I have to go. I have to get help. I'll be back. I promise I'll be back. All right? Can you hear me? Can you say anything?"

Please don't leave me, Cassandra thought desperately, please don't go.

As if in response, the voice replied, "I promise I'll be back, Cassandra. All right? I promise. I have to go. I need to get help."

She didn't have enough strength to cry, but waves of despair and sorrow washed over, drowning her in a feverish daze. The voice was gone. She was alone again. And then everything went blank once more.

∗   ∗   ∗   ∗

"Cassandra?" a voice suddenly asked.

Cassandra was so wrapped up in her haze, so far away, she felt as though she was hearing things from underwater. She'd been asleep again. She fought the urge to close her eyes.

"She can't seem to talk."

"She's probably hurt."

"I'm going down."

"Be careful."

"I will."

"Is the rope tight?"

"Yes, Papa."

"She's been down there for hours."

"Don't worry—we'll get her out."

"Yes, I can do it."

Several voices. There were several voices up there.

Thrashing. Loud thrashing. Endless thrashing. Closer and closer and closer. It sounded like it would never stop.

Then movement. Above her. Nearby. Someone was here! Here in the darkness. With her.

Right beside her. A loud gasp.

"Oh my gosh!" the voice said, and it was right there, right there beside her, and it sounded wretched and sad and miserable. "Your leg…all the blood. Oh, Cassandra."

Were those blue eyes staring at her? Could it be…

She was forced into something tight and rough and pinching and sharp. Cassandra wanted to scream with pain, but no sound escaped from her mouth.

A strong tug and her body went on fire. She was rising, slowly, upward, and the pain was unbearable.

And then, after what seemed like years, she felt the murky darkness finally release her. The air was damp, it was cool, a breeze whispered across her skin. The voices were talking again, and then she heard a strange pounding on the ground, as if someone was running toward her, and all the voices hushed immediately.

"My little girl!" she heard someone cry in a sad, tortured voice. Then it turned to wonder. "You saved my little girl!"

And she heard another voice reply, "I wish I could save more."

Cassandra wanted to see all that she was hearing, but all she could make out was grey movement around her—grey smudges, grey shapes, flurries of grey all around her—and in the middle of it all, a pair of bright green eyes. Oh! Without any thought at all, she grabbed hard in that direction, not knowing from where she'd summoned the strength, and felt herself catch something, and yanked.

"Argh!" a voice cried. "Cassandra, I know you're very happy to see me, but do you have to pull all the hair out of my head?"

It was amazing, but she laughed, or tried to. It didn't sound like a laugh, it sounded more like a horrible grunt, but she was laughing.

He could always make her laugh, even when she was half-delirious with pain.

CHAPTER 20

▼

Another glorious Catskills season had come to an end, and Pop took the stage at the Farewell To Summer Dance to serenade his guests.

Pop's special farewell song, which he sang every year, was a much beloved tradition at The Waterfalls, and even though Pop could no more carry a tune than the cows in the barn, it was the sentiment behind the song that his guests loved.

The dining room was magical—bright-hued paper lanterns at each table and colored ribbons hanging from the ceiling—as The Waterfalls hosted its last event of the summer. Cassandra giggled as Pop's off-key voice rang through the room.

> *Good-bye till next summer,*
> *From the land of the knish,*
> *Where everything tastes better,*
> *Especially with gefilte fish.*

The guests laughed and sang along and wiped their eyes, promising one another they'd return again next year for another Catskills summer of bracing lake water, fat mosquitoes, shuffleboard, and fireflies.

Cassandra sat at a table with Bubbe, Chip, and Esther. Dr. Greenberg had mended her broken leg and other injuries, and she would be fine. She'd spent the last two weeks in bed, and just the other day, had a walking cast put on.

"More tea with honey, *sheyne meydele?*"

"Oh, thank you," Cassandra replied, and Bubbe re-filled her cup. It brought her grandmother so much joy to fuss over her. Cassandra knew Bubbe liked having her granddaughter grounded for a while—no longer able to escape her endless cups of tea and hot bowls of soup. Cassandra felt like she knew nothing of the outside world anymore.

"More herring for you?" Bubbe asked Chip.

"Absolutely," he replied. "I thought you'd never ask."

Bubbe beamed with pleasure. At last she'd found someone with a bottomless stomach—someone who never said no to another helping.

Pop finished his song. The guests rose to their feet and showered him with applause and whistling and hooting. Pop bowed and waved and blew kisses. The band launched into *Cheek to Cheek*. Everyone turned out onto the floor to do the fox trot for one last time this summer.

Esther turned to Cassandra, her sapphire-blue eyes shining with excitement. "Is it all right if I dance with Chip?" she asked, then added in a low voice that wasn't so low that he couldn't overhear her, "Don't worry—I won't try to steal him—he's terribly in love with you!" She said this last part with great admiration.

Cassandra blushed furiously. She glanced at Chip, wondering if he'd heard that. When he winked at her, she realized he'd not only heard it, he'd answered it. *Can't you tell?* He leaned forward and kissed her, right in front of everybody, and Cassandra didn't care who knew or who saw. Thank goodness it wasn't a secret anymore! Bubbe sighed loudly, giving Cassandra a look of part-dreaminess and part-approval.

Chip got up from the table. "May I have this dance?" he asked Esther, holding out his hand.

Esther smiled, but didn't blush or giggle. She gave Chip her hand, and he led her to the dance floor. Cassandra watched the two of them, and felt so happy she wanted to burst. Chip was staying on for the winter, and her best friend wasn't only extraordinarily *mature*, she was speaking to her again. And it hit her. Mama had shown her the way after all. It had been a frightening and painful way, but Mama had done it.

It was Esther who'd crawled down into the ravine to rescue Cassandra. Esther, who could barely climb a tree, who had made it to the bottom of the ravine and back, and with Chip and Uncle Max's help, pulled Cassandra to safety. And it was Pop who'd heard about it, and come running to help. It was their voices she'd heard when she'd been surrounded by all the grey movement.

Pop approached the table. "How are you feeling, *ziskeit*?" he asked.

"Wonderful," she said, and it was true.

He crouched down next to her. "There's something I want to show you, *ziskeit*," he said. "Outside."

Outside? Cassandra glanced at Bubbe, but her grandmother nodded.

This was strange. Bubbe was letting Pop take her outside? Now? Just as the sun was setting? In her condition? *In a walking cast?*

Cassandra leaned against Pop as he helped her outside. The setting sun was brilliant—a fiery orange smear across the horizon. Katydids sang shrilly and ducks quacked on the pond's glossy surface.

Pop steered Cassandra toward the waterfalls. It was treacherously slow going, and Cassandra wondered why Pop was going to such trouble to take her there, but when they reached it, she knew.

"Oh, Pop," she murmured, a lump in her throat.

The fence was gone.

Author's Note

Although most people associate the Golden Age of the Catskills with the 1950s and 1960s—as immortalized in films such as *Dirty Dancing*—it began much earlier, in the 1930s, and that is the time period I chose for my story.

My father-in-law, Leo Friedman, grew up in the Catskills, on a farm/boardinghouse called High Cliff House in Mountaindale, very much like the one in my story.

Although the extravagant hotel resorts always bring to mind the Catskills, there were actually five hundred types of accommodations there, ranging from rustic cabins and crude cottages to weathered bungalow colonies and working farms. Grossinger's and Kutsher's, two fabled hotels, both began as farms. *Kucha-leins*—literally "cook for yourself"—were simple colonies that never got as much attention as the great hotels, but were very popular.

In fact, one reason for the area's tremendous success was that it provided a summer haven for every pocketbook. The wealthy stayed at the renowned hotels—the Concord, Granit, Nevele, Falls View, and Pines. The working class stayed at the more affordable camps, roominghouses, and bungalow colonies.

The fresh air, open space, and beautiful scenery of the Catskills allowed one million New Yorkers to escape blistering summers in the city every year for the cool shade of the mountains. Wives and children usually stayed all summer while fathers, who had jobs back in the city, visited on weekends. This became affectionately known as the "arrival of the Dads."

This mountain region just 90 miles north of New York City was dubbed the Borsht Belt for the red beet soup so popular among its mostly Jewish clientele, and enjoyed a heyday that lasted from the 1930s to the 1960s.

Jewish immigrants came to the Catskills at the turn of the century. The stony soil and short growing season were difficult, so many began hosting friends who were eager to escape city summers.

Regardless of how lavish or modest, hotels went to great lengths to please their guests. *Tummlers* created elaborate social programs and legendary entertainment. Many world-famous entertainers got their start in the Catskills: Mel Brooks, Joan Rivers, Barbra Streisand, Lucille Ball, Rodney Dangerfield, Sid Caesar, Red Buttons, Ed Sullivan, Sammy Davis Jr., Jackie Mason, the Marx brothers, Tony Curtis, Milton Berle, Alan King, Danny Kaye, and Jerry Lewis.

Guests usually returned to the same hotel year after year, and whole New York neighborhoods sometimes lodged together. These summer resorts were not merely hotels and colonies, but miniature societies where people created intricate relationships with one another. These New York Jews created a whole world shaped by their music, humor, language, food, and outlook.

It was a time characterized by a great sense of belonging, a great sense of community, an endless summer connection that was close-knit and unforgettable. Jews could become Americanized while preserving their Jewishness. They could have a proper vacation like regular Americans, but they could do it in a very Jewish way.

The distinctive culture of the Catskills has been celebrated in several films, including *Marjorie Morningstar*, *A Walk on the Moon*, *Sweet Lorraine*, and, as mentioned earlier, *Dirty Dancing*.

Despite its immense popularity, however, the Catskills would die a lingering death in the four decades between the 1960s and the present day. The invention of air conditioning made New York summers more bearable, and television offered entertainment at home. Affordable airline travel lured people to Europe and other exotic destinations.

Jews who'd grown up in Europe wanted nothing more than to escape it, especially after the horrors of the Holocaust and World War II. But the newer Jewish generation was curious about the world, and wanted to see it. And they were better educated, more affluent, more Americanized, and less interested in vacationing Jewishly. As one hotel owner lamented, "I used to compete with the hotel down the road. Now I compete with the world."

Today, the Catskills is a sad series of ghost towns—decaying buildings, rusting billboards, faded signs, swimming pools overrun with weeds, and screened porches festooned with cobwebs. Most of the famous hotels have shut down.

Many political leaders have tried to re-energize the Catskills. Some have proposed gambling and casinos; the St. Regis Mohawk Indian tribe has expressed interest. And many of today's New Yorkers are "discovering" the Catskills as a summer alternative to the Hamptons.

But the special time, place, and culture of the Catskills is gone forever, alive only in the memories of those who were lucky enough to have been a part of it.

Glossary of Yiddish Words

Bubbe	grandmother
Chuppah	wedding canopy
Chutzpah	the nerve
Derma	type of homemade sausage
Druchus	the sticks
Es vet gornit helfen	nothing will help
Ess gezunterhait	eat in good health
Farshtaist	you understand?
Feh	yuck
Flanken	type of meat dish
Folg mich	obey me
Haimish	warm, friendly
Kasha varnishkes	bowtie pasta with buckwheat groats
Kibitz	gossip
Kreplach	dumpling
Kugel	a noodle pudding
Luft	fresh air
Mandlebrot	crunchy biscotti-like bread

Mandlen	soup nuts
Mensch	decent, good person
Meshugah	crazy
Nudnik	pest
Oy gevalt	oh, no
Pitseler	small child
Rugelach	jam-filled pastry squares
Se shtinkt	it stinks
Shadchan	matchmaker
Shanda	disgrace
Sheyne medele	pretty face
Shtetl	village, ghetto
Tatte	father
Tsu gezunt	you're welcome
Tummler	social director
Tzimmes	a vegetable pudding
Um-be-shrien	it shouldn't happen
Vai is mir	woe is me
Verklempt	on verge of tears
Vos iz der tachlis	what's the purpose?
Vos noch	what then?
Zeyde	grandfather
Ziskeit	little child

Bibliography

Brown, Phil, *In the Catskills: A Century of the Jewish Experience in the Mountains*, Columbia University Press, 2002.

Brown, Phil, *Catskill Culture: A Mountain Rat's Memories of the Great Jewish Resort Area*, Temple University Press, 1998.

Kanfer, Stefan, *A Summer World: The Attempt to Build A Jewish Eden in the Catskills*, Farrar, Straus & Giroux, 1989.

McElvaine, Robert S., *The Great Depression: America 1929–1941*, Three Rivers Press, 1993.

Richman, Irwin, *Borscht Belt Bungalows: Memories of Catskill Summers*, Temple University Press, 1998.

Watkins, T.H., *The Great Depression: America in the 1930s*, Little, Brown and Company, 1999.

Here's a Sneak Peek at *The Necklace*,
the sequel to *The Fence*, coming soon!

Chapter 1

She was the love of his life.

And she deserved the most wonderful birthday present in the world.

So, Chip panicked in front of the glass display case at Bernstein's.

Cassandra's seventeenth birthday was three days away and he still hadn't found anything for her. He certainly couldn't buy her a comic book, puzzle, bobby pins, or candy. He wanted something special, something *big*, something that wasn't at the local five-and-ten.

The redhead behind the counter peered at him eagerly. She'd been trying to catch his eye for the last ten minutes.

"Can I help you find what you're looking for?" she finally asked in a voice dripping with sweetness and with russet-hued eyelashes fluttering at full throttle.

"I'm looking for a birthday present for my girlfriend," he replied, keeping his eyes on the glass display case.

"Your girlfriend?" she exclaimed none too subtly. Then, regaining her composure, she observed tartly, "Well, I guess she's the type that's hard to buy for, see, I'm the type that's easy to buy for." She fluttered her rosy eyelashes some more.

Chip looked at her. She was young. Probably his age—eighteen. And she was pretty—very pretty. But Cassandra was the most beautiful girl in the world.

"You'll make some fellow very happy," he said.

"I could make *you* very happy," she responded with a nervous giggle.

He smiled. "I'm sure you could. But I'm already very happy."

She sighed, giving up. "She's an awfully lucky girl."

"Actually, I'm a lucky guy."

It was time to end this conversation. Chip grabbed a package of black licorice whips off the candy rack and reached into his pocket to pay for them. The redhead gave him her hand and their fingers brushed as he dropped his coins into it. He gave her another smile and left the store. She stared after him longingly.

Chip passed Smiley's bar, Godlin's pharmacy, Dill's hardware store, and the Centre Theater movie house, where the marquee announced the film *Conquest* starring Greta Garbo. He'd already spent an hour in Woodbourne, and if he didn't get back soon, Cassandra would wonder about him. The only things he'd accomplished in that hour were satisfying his urge for a chocolate egg cream at the soda fountain inside Lebed's pharmacy, catching up on the news of November 12, 1937 by reading a newspaper some fellow had left on the counter, and finishing his latest book, *The Great Gatsby*.

Why had he spent money on that egg cream? Now he had less to spend on Cassandra's birthday present. He shouldn't have bought the black licorice whips either. But he felt he had to buy something at Bernstein's, and he was hungry, stupidly forgetting to bring a sandwich from Bubbe's bountiful kitchen. He'd try Monticello tomorrow. It was a bigger town with a department store. And he'd bring something to eat, so he wouldn't waste more money.

He reached the end of downtown and walked along the road. The frost was late this year and many of the trees still held their leaves. He admired the brilliant explosion of rich crimsons, golds, and oranges. The Catskills were beautiful in the fall—the mountain air as crisp and clear as cold well water.

He'd hitchhiked to Woodbourne and hoped he could get another ride back quickly. Luckily, a truck piled with wooden crates full of squawking hens stopped for him. White feathers tumbled out like fat snow flakes. The farmer turned out to be a talkative type. By the time they'd reached Mountaindale and The Waterfalls, Chip knew everything there was to know about raising prize-winning Leghorns.

Chip thanked the farmer and jogged toward the hotel. Cassandra ran across the pasture to greet him, her thick dark hair flapping behind her. He braced himself—she'd knocked him over two weeks ago. Thankfully, they'd been in the barn, and he'd fallen backward into a hill of soft hay. And Cassandra had laughed her head off as they untangled themselves from a jumble of entwined arms and legs. Chip loved that about her. She laughed at everything, even his jokes, especially the stupid ones.

He was ready for her, though, when she flew into him. He caught her in his arms and gave her a long, slow kiss. He admired her dark eyes and beautiful hair, and told her he loved her, and waited for her to tell him the same thing, as she usually did, but, instead, she exclaimed, her eyes shining with excitement, "Your parents are coming!"

Look for *The Necklace*.
Coming Soon.

978-0-595-37220-1
0-595-37220-1

CPSIA information can be obtained at www.ICGtesting.com
Printed in the USA
LVOW041946070812

293337LV00014B/10/A